BBC

DOCTOR WHO

With thanks to
Professor Joel Christensen of Brandeis University

BBC CHILDREN'S BOOKS
UK | USA | Canada | Ireland | Australia
India | New Zealand | South Africa
BBC Children's Books are published by Puffin Books,
part of the Penguin Random House group of companies
whose addresses can be found at global.penguinrandomhouse.com.
www.penguin.co.uk   www.puffin.co.uk   www.ladybird.co.uk

Penguin
Random House
UK

First published 2020
001

Written by David Solomons
Cover illustrations by Beatriz Castro
Text illustrations by George Ermos
Copyright © BBC, 2020

BBC, Doctor Who and TARDIS (word marks and logos)
are trade marks of the British Broadcasting
Corporation and are used under licence.
BBC logo © BBC 1996. Doctor Who logo © BBC 2018.
Licensed by BBC Studios.

Set in 13/16pt Sabon LT Std
Typeset by Jouve (UK), Milton Keynes
Printed and bound in Great Britain by Clays Ltd, Elcograf S.p.A.
A CIP catalogue record for this book is available from the British Library

ISBN: 978–1–405–93762–7

All correspondence to:
BBC Children's Books
Penguin Random House Children's UK
One Embassy Gardens, New Union Square,
5 Nine Elms Lane, London SW8 5DA

BBC

DOCTOR WHO

THE MAZE OF DOOM

DAVID SOLOMONS

Cover illustrations by Beatriz Castro

Text illustrations by George Ermos

PUFFIN

For my daughter, Lara, who's on course
to be the Twentieth Doctor.

Contents

1. Too Close to the Sun

Island of Crete, circa 2000 BC

Icarus watched the flying orb touch the edge of the setting sun and explode into flames. With jarring suddenness, it altered course, and fell to Earth trailing fire.

He flinched at the violence that had shattered the peace of the late afternoon. He and his father had come to the beach, as they had done every evening, to chart the heavens. They had spent the summer of this, Icarus's fifteenth year, noting the position and motion of the celestial objects that speckled the curtain of night. At first, Icarus had believed the fast-moving orb he'd

1

sighted low in the western sky to be a falling star. Sitting beneath the clear night skies of their island homeland, wrapped up against the cold, they had recorded several such phenomena already this year. He knew that many of his countrymen feared the blazing light in the dark. They regarded it as a bad omen signifying the death of a king, or the coming of a natural disaster. For others, it was more than a portent – it was a god falling from the sky. Icarus didn't believe in any of that stuff. His father had taught him to approach the world with a critical mind, so Icarus dismissed all these explanations as superstitious nonsense.

He tracked the object with sharp, youthful eyes. As it sank lower, the orb came more clearly into view. From here it looked more disc than orb, and huge – thousands of cubits wide, bigger than the king's palace at Knossos. The very air shuddered at its passage, while shafts of golden sunlight rolled off its smooth surfaces, gleaming like the throne in the same palace.

Beside him, Icarus heard his father gasp and mutter, 'By the gods, what is it?'

The words made Icarus afraid. His father, Daedalus, the man of reason, was calling on the very gods he spurned. But Icarus understood his father's fear and wonder. The object was too perfect to be found in nature; it had to be the work of humankind. Or god. Some kind of vessel.

A ship of the sky.

It fell without a sound, and then was gone, dipping from sight beyond a rocky outcrop at the far end of the shoreline.

As Icarus ran up the beach for a better vantage, he heard a resounding boom, like the sound that the crumbling cliffs had made the year before when they had tumbled into the sea. By the time he'd reached higher ground, the setting sun had all but disappeared. A pale finger of light pointed to the skyship's watery resting place. The wine-dark sea bubbled and boiled around the spot, while something vast and otherworldly glimmered beneath the surface.

News of the crash quickly reached the palace. Word came that the king himself would ride out to inspect the mysterious object for himself. In the morning, Icarus watched a group of figures approaching fast across the beach: the king at the head of a detachment of royal cavalry, bronze helmets flashing in the early sun, their mounts' hooves skimming the sand. They were an awe-inspiring spectacle. However, he knew that they were as nothing to the spectacle that awaited them.

3

Icarus turned to look out to sea. The tide had receded, exposing the fallen skyship. It was like the shield of some war god, half buried in the shallows, its shadow darkening the shoreline. He shivered in the morning air.

At first, the procession swept past the gawping Icarus, but then the king reined in his horse and trotted back towards him, the royal mount kicking up clods of sand. With a snort, it came to a halt, so close that Icarus could see the sheen of sweat on its flanks. Astride the horse, King Minos of Crete gazed down upon him.

'Boy, where is your father?'

Daedalus was the king's most trusted adviser. King Minos went to him for advice on matters astronomical, medical, architectural, sculptural, musical and political. In fact, the king rarely made a decision about anything without first consulting Daedalus.

Icarus swallowed. His mouth felt as dry as the sand he shuffled his feet on.

'Where's your tongue?' King Minos snapped. 'Answer me, before I have it cut out.'

Kings were not known for their patience.

The truth was that natural curiosity had overcome Daedalus and, as dawn arrived, he and Icarus had ventured closer to the stricken skyship, the better to inspect the vessel. Wading out into the shallows, they had found a broken seam in the otherwise unblemished exterior, like an armoured breastplate pierced by a well-placed arrow. The split was wide enough to squeeze through, giving access to the ship's interior. It was too tempting to resist. Instructing his son to stay put, Daedalus had gone inside.

That had been several hours ago.

Before Icarus could convey any of this, the captain of the guard's voice trembled on the morning air.

'Sire, look there!' He thrust out an arm.

All eyes turned to where he pointed. At the base of the vessel, where the shining hull met the sand, a section was opening up. Icarus would have called it a door, except that it was bigger than any door he had ever seen, dwarfing even the entrance to the great temple. No human needed a door that big.

And it was no human that emerged.

It had the broad head and legs of a bull and stood some ten cubits tall, yet seemed even taller thanks to two great horns that sprang from its head. It regarded the Minoan welcome party with a pair of blazing red eyes.

'Great Zeus,' muttered the king.

'Protect the king!' cried the captain of the guard.

Responding to this call, two of the king's men drew their swords and urged their mounts forward to intercept the creature.

It sensed their approach. Cloven hooves pawing at the sand, the beast lowered its head. Icarus expected it to charge like any other bull, but instead it pointed the twin horns at the cavalry.

A spiral of light leaped from its horns, as red as the creature's terrible eyes. As the vivid beam touched the leading soldier, he let out a scream. His cry was cut short as his flesh turned to ashes and his bones fell to the ground. The bodily remains of the soldier drifted away on the breeze, as his horse fled, unscathed.

The surviving soldier had closed the distance between himself and the creature to a few horse-lengths.

It swung its head to aim at the onrushing horse and rider. Its movements were unsteady and ponderous, causing Icarus to wonder if it had been injured in the crash.

The cavalry blade flashed in the sunlight. With a howl of pain, the bull creature went down, clutching its shoulder. Thick black blood gouted from the freshly inflicted wound on to the pristine sand. The creature sank to its knees. Seemingly exhausted and no longer a threat, it emitted a keening sound as though it was in pain.

The soldier jumped down from his horse and raised his sword once more, ready to deliver the killing blow and avenge his fallen comrade. His furious grip tightened round the hilt. Just then, the bull creature opened one of its strangely human hands, revealing in its leathery palm a device the size and shape of a large coin. Before the soldier could react, the device exploded, flinging tiny shards through the air. The soldier winced in pain, clutching a hand to one eye, where a fragment of the disintegrating device had struck. He shrugged off the injury – just a scratch.

'Sire!' yelled a voice.

Icarus shaded his eyes from the low sun and attempted to locate the source of the familiar voice. It was Daedalus, calling from the open door of the skyship. He carried something across one arm. It looked like a warrior's shield, and for a moment Icarus thought it must be, but he dismissed that idea just as swiftly as it had arisen. His father was many things, but a warrior was not one of them.

King Minos trotted forward, and in his wake Icarus crept closer. The king paused over the injured creature. It snorted like a bull of the field, but its breaths came shallow and its blood soaked the sand. With one last bellow, it slumped to the ground and breathed no longer.

'Is it dead?' the king asked tentatively.

Daedalus lowered the round shield-like object, dropped to the ground and made a cursory inspection, before announcing, 'I believe so, Your Majesty.'

The king drew his own sword and gave the beast an investigative poke. 'What abomination is this?'

Daedalus shook his head in wonder. 'It came from the stars.'

'Sent by the gods?'

Daedalus made a pained expression.

'Yes, yes,' tutted the king. 'But unlike you, my enlightened friend, the rest of my subjects will believe that this is a judgement from the gods. The people must not learn of this *thing*. Burn it.'

'No!'

The king glared at him. 'You dare defy me?'

'With your indulgence, I would like to study the creature.' Daedalus gestured to the skyship. 'And its vessel. I have been inside and it is . . .' He struggled for words. 'Wondrous. There is much we can learn. Much we can take.'

This stirred the king's interest. 'Gold? Jewels?'

'Something greater than either,' declared Daedalus. 'I found this after only a short exploration of the interior.' He lifted up the object Icarus had believed to be a shield. Apart from a small central section, its surface was featureless.

Holding it horizontally, Daedalus let go, but instead of falling to the ground the object remained in place, floating like a feather upon the wind.

'I believe it is a flying machine,' said Daedalus, gazing at it in awe.

In the stunned silence that followed, Icarus was aware of an odd repetitive sound. Above the distant lapping of the waves he could make it out quite clearly.

Tick-tick-tick.

It was coming from the centre of the shield. He saw now that the central part – what would be called the boss on a soldier's shield – was embedded with an intricate mesh of wheels. Each wheel had a circumference of tiny teeth that interlocked with the next wheel.

'And this is just the beginning,' Daedalus went on excitedly. 'We have been granted access to a treasure trove.'

The king appeared to weigh his words. Slowly he looked up at the towering skyship and then back to Daedalus. 'Very well. But hide your work from ordinary eyes. The people will call this a bad omen. Kings and omens do not sit well together.' He snapped his reins and rejoined his men. The cavalry formed up around him and they rode off across the beach.

Icarus regarded the ship and its occupant. 'He asks you to hide a mountain. Father, how is it possible?'

There was a gleam in Daedalus's eyes. Icarus knew this look. His father was deep in thought. He tucked the mysterious flying machine under one arm and steered the boy towards the skyship's open hatch. 'Now, let's get you out of the sun.'

Tick-tick-tick . . .

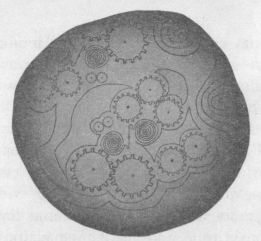

2. Out of the Blue

Unfashionable end of the Western spiral arm of the galaxy, circa 2020 AD

Alone in the dimly lit console room, the clicks and whirs of the timeship's baffling control mechanisms filling the air, Yasmin Khan caught herself.

She was aboard an *actual* alien spaceship.

There was rarely time to reflect on her remarkable circumstances, what with running along endless corridors, fending off crazed Stenza warriors and helping to save the universe on a weekly basis. So, when an opportunity arose to reflect on her journey, she seized the chance.

The viewscreen showed the constellation of stars through which they were currently travelling. She watched them hang in the darkness of the void. They didn't twinkle out here – she'd learned it was the passage of their light through the Earth's atmosphere that made them appear to do that. Not that the view was any less awe-inspiring for that. And, somewhere out there among them, was her home. Her mind flew back to another time and place. She pictured her younger self sitting at a desk in Redlands Primary School, carefully writing out her address as part of some lame exercise set by her teacher. Yaz had always constructed it the same way:

Yasmin Khan
Flat 34
Park Hill
Sheffield
England
United Kingdom
Europe
The World
The Milky Way
The Universe

Now, as she stood at the heart of the astonishing ship, she realised that wasn't just her address – it was her journey. A schoolgirl in Sheffield, a probationary police constable for Hallamshire Police and now ... Who was she exactly? Astronaut? Explorer? Assistant saviour of the universe? *Who?* Her brief spell with the mysterious traveller known as the Doctor had already granted her more experience of life, the universe and everything than she could have dreamed, but it wasn't half going to be tricky to describe on a CV.

BLINK. BLINK.

The orange light on the display ticked on and off with the regularity of a car indicator, but it promised something far more interesting than a left turn into Talbot Street.

It was a distress signal.

Since joining the Doctor on her travels, Yaz had got used to racing across time and space to the aid of some alien race/marooned humanoids/ sentient vegetables/all of the above. But there was something notably different about this signal. Unlike every call for help they'd received so far, this one had originated from *inside the ship*.

That wouldn't have been a problem in an ordinary vessel, but this one was far from ordinary. It was called the TARDIS (or, more accurately, *a* TARDIS, although Yaz had yet to encounter another). The letters formed an acronym that stood for Time And Relative Dimension In Space. Which, frankly, was meaningless mumbo-jumbo. In practice, it meant the ship mucked about with your perception of scale. So, on the outside, the TARDIS appeared to be a regular blue police box from Earth's mid-twentieth century, but one turn of its disappointingly ordinary key opened the doors into a room your monkey brain told you couldn't possibly fit inside the modest exterior dimensions. Yaz could only compare it to one of those Russian-doll sets, where you opened the first wooden doll to find a smaller one inside, and so on and so on. It was like that, except imagine opening up the first Russian doll and finding Russia.

Taken Aback Regarding Disorientating InSides. That was more like it.

The first place you encountered was this, the console room. A command bridge, although that seemed somewhat grand for a vessel whose flight controls included a custard-cream dispenser. But the console room was just the beginning. The TARDIS wasn't big. The Meadowhall shopping centre was big. The TARDIS was unfathomable. A maze of corridors and doors, decks and staircases, walk-in wardrobes and ballrooms. Apparently, there was even a swimming pool somewhere. Not only was the ship a confusing labyrinth, but to make matters worse it also had a personality. Annoyingly, most of the time it seemed to Yaz to have the personality of a ten-year-old boy, and liked to keep its crewmembers guessing. Yaz could have sworn that it constantly rejigged the interior layout, moving walls and doors so that, even after living aboard for as long as she had, she would still get lost. She could never find the loo in the middle of the night. In an odd way, the ship wasn't so different from the Doctor herself – playful, puzzling and, occasionally, downright reckless. As she thought about it, Yaz realised that she couldn't picture one without the other. The Doctor and the TARDIS were inextricably linked.

Right now, the TARDIS was playing one of its games – hide-and-seek, to be exact. Yaz and the others had spent hours searching for the source of the distress signal. If it wanted to, the TARDIS could presumably have led them right to it, but instead it was pranking them. She could almost hear it chuckling into its chocolate milk at their attempts to locate the signal's origin. At some point, she had grown weary of the game and decided to come here to the console room for a break.

She cast her eyes across the befuddling main console. It was hexagonal in shape, requiring six qualified members of crew to pilot it successfully. But, since the Doctor was the only one among them to have the foggiest idea about how to steer the thing, every flight involved her running around the console like a kid in a playground. The main scanner in the wall next to the console displayed exterior images. More panels provided information that assisted the Doctor in navigating time and space – or at least gave the impression that she was moderately in charge of the process. Yaz saw that Graham had left his sandwich maker plugged into the console, so she took the opportunity to make herself a cheese toastie. She fired up the Breville and waited.

Usually, the Doctor would be throwing switches and hauling levers and the place would be rocking and buffeting its way through time and space to a new adventure on an alien world. Or Sheffield. But for now it was relatively quiet. Yaz laid a palm on the surface of the console. The material was paradoxically cool and warm at the same time, and it pulsed beneath her fingers as if alive. It was not like anything she had encountered on Earth. Back home, she had been in training to be a police officer. A thought popped into her head: a cop with a time machine, solving crimes across the universe. That'd make a great TV show. Her mum would watch the heck out of that. She fished out her toastie, nibbled the piping-hot snack and imagined herself in the starring role, confronting some alien horror using her particular set of skills.

'Excuse me, madam, but are you aware that the rear offside light on your flying saucer is broken?' She mimed a quick-draw, holding out the half-eaten sandwich like a gun. 'Keep your tentacles where I can see them!'

'Ahem.'

Yaz spun round to see a woman in a grey gabardine coat, which was open to reveal a rainbow-patterned top and blue dungarees. Her short blonde bob was partially concealed beneath a knitted hat in the shape of a chicken. Two strings dangled loosely from either side of the hat, ending in bobbles of red yarn.

'Sorry,' said the Doctor, wrinkling her nose apologetically. 'Didn't mean to sneak up on you when you were . . .' She paused, putting her head on one side. 'What *were* you doing?'

'Nothing.' Yaz lowered her sandwich with as much dignity as she could muster.

'Were you pretending to be the star of your own cop show?' asked the Doctor. 'Because that's a brilliant idea!' She extended one hand and drew it slowly across her chest, declaring in a gravelly voice, 'In a world on fire, only one

woman and her plucky canine companion . . .'
She paused. 'I feel your character should have a
dog.' The Doctor's gaze drifted off and her
knitted bobbles swung gently from side to side.
'I had a canine companion once.'

Yaz knew so little about the Doctor's past –
mostly because there was such a lot of it.
'Labrador? Poodle?'

'Robot.' Her shoulders heaved with a sigh.

Yaz had reconciled herself to being surprised
on a regular basis by this kind of thing. After all,
anyone who had lived as long as the Doctor was
bound to have accumulated a lot of baggage.
And she was properly old. Although the woman
in front of her appeared to be somewhere in her
thirties, Yaz knew that she was on the far side
of two thousand. Yaz had learned that such
longevity wasn't unusual for someone like the
Doctor, who came from the planet Gallifrey. Far
beyond the Milky Way, located in the constellation
of Kasterborous, was the planet of the Time
Lords, a race of spacefaring, dimension-hopping,
giant-collar-wearing beings who'd mastered the
mechanics of time travel (up to a point). An
inscrutable people with a fearsome intellect,
guardians of the secrets of the universe and –

'D'you like my chicken hat?' asked the Doctor.

And fans of novelty headwear. Apparently.

18

'Thought I'd lost it. Pressie from the Master-Weavers of Arnn after I helped them out with a nasty double cross-stitch. They gave me this and the secret to the reverse triple-crochet.' She tugged at the cords dangling from the hat. The chicken's wings flapped and its beak opened wide.

It was a peculiarly elegant action, thought Yaz.

The Doctor examined the blinking light on the console, tapping it lightly. 'Found my knitted chicken, but still don't know where you're coming from.'

As she made several minor adjustments to the controls, there was a commotion from the entrance to the console room and two men sprinted inside. One young and black, the other older and white, both out of breath. They skidded to a stop and Yaz considered them as they recovered. Ryan Sinclair and Graham O'Brien were an unlikely duo, neither as dynamic as Batman and Robin nor as ideally matched as fish and chips. Their history may not have been as ancient as the Doctor's, but it contained more than enough anguish and sorrow. Flung together as a blended family of grandfather and grandson aboard the TARDIS, they had been initially scratchy with each other but mortal danger and monsters had brought them close.

Graham stood bent over, hands on his knees, gulping for air after his dash through the TARDIS. The younger man, Ryan, recovered first and held up what looked to Yaz like a small, crumpled paper bag. With a grin he announced, 'Found it! This is what's been sending out the signal.'

'Doesn't look very distressed,' Yaz noted.

'Quick,' urged Graham through ragged breaths. 'Give it to the Doc!'

Ryan thrust the bag at her. The Doctor looked puzzled. 'Why the rush?'

Graham stood up with a confused expression. 'Aren't we racing against time, with the fate of all life in the galaxy at stake?'

The Doctor exchanged a glance with Yaz, who shrugged her shoulders. 'Uh, no.'

'Oh.' Graham puffed out. 'Then, you're also out of hand soap in the toilet next to the swimming pool.'

Yaz beamed. 'You found the pool!'

While Graham attempted to describe to Yaz precisely how to reach the semi-mythical pool, the Doctor took the bag from Ryan. The paper was yellowing and brittle with age.

'Found it in the pocket of an old coat,' said Ryan.

The Doctor raised a flap of her hat and lifted the bag to her ear. 'It's ticking.'

'Bomb?' asked Ryan nervously.

The Doctor shook the bag curiously, much to the consternation of the others.

'Don't shake the bomb!' cried Graham.

'Not really a bomb-y kind of tick,' said the Doctor. 'More clock-y.' She tipped up the bag and half a dozen small human-shaped figurines fell into her open palm, alongside a roughly circular lump of grey-green stone that was the size of a large coin and embedded with what appeared to be a series of tiny interlocking gears.

Graham plucked one of the figurines between thumb and forefinger and examined it with the concentration of a jeweller appraising a diamond. 'The carving's primitive, the figures appear to be childlike . . . I'd guess ceremonial in nature . . .'

'Very funny, Graham,' said the Doctor, taking a Jelly Baby and banging it against the TARDIS console. 'Petrified.' She turned to Ryan. 'The coat where you found this – was it by any chance hanging next to a five-metre-long stripy scarf?'

'Yeah,' said Ryan, gesturing to the ticking stone. 'So, d'you know what it is then?'

'Haven't the foggiest. But I was always picking up random stuff back then.'

Back then, thought Yaz. That was another thing the Time Lords had mastered. Immortality – or extreme longevity. She hadn't seen it for herself, but from what she understood the Doctor had the ability to regenerate her physical body, transferring her consciousness, mostly intact, to a new body. So if she suffered a mortal injury, for instance, she could hop into a box-fresh bod. Which was nice. Yaz realised that the Doctor was making a reference to one of her past lives, the coat and scarf presumably belonging to an earlier regeneration.

It was only then that Yaz noticed that the gears in the stone were moving. Cog by cog it turned, a perfect symphony of revolving parts. Whatever this thing was, the mechanism was intact – and strangely beautiful.

'Let's find out what you are,' mused the Doctor and, slotting the stone into a space on the console, she threw a handful of switches and spun several dials. 'It appears to be some kind of engine. But what's making it tick? Where's the power coming from?'

'The TARDIS?' offered Ryan.

'The TARDIS uses artron energy. This thing is powered by a garden variety of electrical energy. I'll try to lock down the source –'

There was a flash from the console, then a sharp burning smell.

'An energy spike.' The Doctor scoured the damaged controls. 'As if something very powerful was switched on and then quickly off again.'

'Can you tell where it came from?' asked Yaz.

The Doctor shook her head. 'It's gone.' She paused, still peering at the console displays. 'Hello, what's this? There's another signal. Nothing like as strong as the first one, but I should be able to track it.' The Doctor slapped a switch, kicked a pedal and the console trilled. She stood back with a triumphant air. 'Earth, around ten years after I picked you lot up.'

'Why's it doing that?' asked Ryan, pointing.

The stone was vibrating in the slot where the Doctor had inserted it in the console. The ticking grew louder.

'Okay, now that *is* bomb-y,' said the Doctor. 'Everyone take cov–'

Before she could complete her warning, there was a flash and a bang. Momentarily blinded, Yaz felt a searing heat and her face was peppered with tiny, hard fragments.

She opened her eyes to see the console room wreathed in smoke and her friends in various states of disarray. The spot on the console where

23

the stone had sat was remarkably undamaged, save for some charring. However, the stone had completely disintegrated. Yaz checked herself out – no obvious damage. The same was true of the Doctor and Graham. She searched the clearing smoke for the fourth member of their team. 'Ryan, you okay?'

He lay on the floor, dazed but conscious, clutching one side of his face and moaning.

'Ryan!' Yaz hurried over and kneeled down beside him.

Graham rushed to join them. 'Oh, god! Ryan, son! Can you see? How many fingers am I holding up?'

Ryan raised himself to a sitting position. 'None. You're not holding up any fingers.'

'Oh, right. Sorry. I panicked.'

Yaz eased Ryan's hand away from his head. Blood trickled from a small cut beneath his left eye. She breathed a sigh of relief. It could've been a lot worse. 'You're okay. Just a scratch. But let's get you cleaned up.'

The Doctor stood over the console, furiously working the controls. 'Something overloaded the engine, causing it to explode, but the TARDIS muffled the blast. Judging by these numbers, if it had gone off in the open we'd be looking at a yield of twenty megatons.'

'A yield of . . .' said Yaz, shocked. 'You mean, like a nuclear weapon?'

The Doctor glanced at Ryan. 'I'm sorry. I should've been more careful.'

'Doc, what're you doing?' asked Graham.

'Being more careful.' She flung a lever and the time-rotor began its rise and fall.

3. Nimon of Athens

London, United Kingdom, circa 2028 AD

The first thing that greeted them on stepping out of the TARDIS was a chorus of chirps, bongs and temple bells emanating from Yaz and Ryan's mobile phones. Disorientated by the trip through time and space, the phones latched on to familiar networks and ravenously sucked down messages and updates. In purely chronological terms it had been ten years since they were last connected, which meant a lot of spam.

'Cool,' said Ryan, noting the top message on the display. 'I'm due five upgrades.'

Graham did not share the younger pair's interest. He had lost his phone at some point during their travels – he suspected it happened during a bumpy journey across the frozen wastes of Calufrax Minor on a sledge pulled by giant snow-bunnies. As the others studied their handsets, he took in their surroundings.

It was London, all right. A row of street lights showed that the TARDIS had materialised at the corner of a wide road junction in what looked like the West End. Red double-decker buses trawled up and down dedicated lanes, cars thrummed past and the wail of police sirens floated on the warm night air. They were outside a grand white stucco building. Neoclassical pillars lined its facade like soldiers at attention, and lights blazed in rows of pleasingly proportioned windows.

'Where are we?' asked Yaz. 'Looks posh.'

'Palace of Whitehall,' said the Doctor. 'At least the only part of it still standing in your era. Last time I was here, they'd just beheaded Charles the First – right about there.' She indicated the spot on the pavement that Graham occupied. He swallowed and took a step to one side. The Doctor breezed past, heading for the building's entrance. 'Whatever overloaded our battery, we are seconds away from discovering it.'

27

They made it as far as the entrance hall before her prediction proved to be over-optimistic, their path barred by a pair of unsmiling security guards bulging out of tight-fitting suit jackets. Past the men, at the end of an arched corridor lit by candelabra, lay a set of double doors, and beyond those the source of the mysterious power signal. But for now the answer was tantalisingly out of reach.

'May I see your invitation?' asked the first guard. It was a toss-up as to which was shinier: his shoes or his bald head.

Graham knew that of course they had no invitation, but that never stopped the Doctor. Like a close-up magician at the climax of a trick, she opened her hand with a flourish and there on her palm lay what looked like a plain plastic wallet. Flipping it open to reveal a seemingly blank pad of white paper, she held it in front of the man's suspicious eyes.

The two guards squinted at the paper, their expressions slowly altering from wariness to acceptance. Graham had seen this happen – a lot. The wallet contained psychic paper, a Time Lord invention that showed whatever the holder wanted the viewer to see. Usually. Some people and alien races had the power to see through the deception, but it was clear to Graham that the guards were no match. As far as their brains were telling them, they were looking at an official invitation.

'This lot are my plus-three,' said the Doctor, thumbing over her shoulder at the others.

'You still can't come in,' snapped the bald guard.

'Why not?' said the Doctor, already angling to go past him.

He turned the blank pad round. 'See what it says right here?'

'Uhh . . .'

'Black tie,' added the guard helpfully. He cast a disapproving glance at the group, ending on Ryan's feet. 'And he's wearing trainers.'

Graham could tell that the Doctor was weighing up her options. Either she could attempt to argue her way past these guys or –

'We'll be right back,' she said and, spinning on her heel, led the others quickly back out on to the pavement and into the TARDIS.

As well as swimming pools, ballrooms and all the rest, the ship contained a voluminous walk-in wardrobe. It was more like a costume department, thought Graham as he searched racks of era-appropriate suits. *Moss Bros in the cosmos.* He squeezed into a traditional black tuxedo and went to look for a mirror. He found Ryan hogging one, admiring his own choice of outfit. The young man had picked a dinner suit in a deep shade of purple.

'You look like an aubergine,' said Graham.

Ryan gave a tug at his sleeves. 'I am rocking this suit.' He was used to his granddad's ribbing, but right now nothing could burst his bubble. He hadn't felt this good in ages. He wasn't sure what had caused the uplift, and he didn't question it too closely. All he knew was that he was buzzing. He adjusted his bow tie in the mirror. There was a gleam in his eye.

He peered closer at his reflection. Yes, there it was. An actual gleam in his left eye. Maybe a fragment of that exploding stone battery thing had got in there? But, if so, why wasn't it bothering him? A piece of grit like that would be irritating, if not downright painful, but he felt better than ever.

Before he could wonder any more about it, on the other side of the room the curtain of a dressing cubicle swept back and the Doctor and Yaz emerged in each other's arms. It took Ryan a moment to realise that they were dancing. The Doctor was leading. She was wearing a jumpsuit in a striking rust colour.

'Nice togs,' said Ryan admiringly.

'I love getting dressed up for a mission,' the Doctor said. 'It's by one of my favourite Zygon designers. No fiddly buttons, but the suckers do leave a mark.'

Yaz was in a long silver dress with a pattern like ripples on a moonlit pond.

'Ready?' asked the Doctor.

'Dip me,' replied Yaz.

The dancers came out of a turn, the Doctor twirled Yaz, then pulled her close, wrapped one hand firmly round her waist, cradled her neck with the other and gently lowered her to the floor as Yaz hugged the Doctor's shoulder.

There was a long silence as they stayed like that for several seconds.

'We should probably go now,' said Yaz.

'Yeah,' agreed the Doctor.

Second time round, they swept past the security guards and made their way swiftly along the candelabra-lit corridor, through the double doors and into what was a striking main hall. Graham took in the white fluted pillars that lined both sides of the soaring space, supporting a gallery that ran the whole way round the room, under a ceiling frescoed with fat babies and blokes in floaty robes. The glow from four low-hanging chandeliers reflected gold flecks in the ceiling and on the tops of the pillars, and shed warm light on the well-heeled guests who occupied the dozens of white-clothed round tables that reached across the polished floor like stepping stones.

'It's a double-cube,' said the Doctor. 'All the room's proportions are mathematically related to create a harmonious whole. The order is pleasing to the human mind, but it'll drive a Yeti nuts.'

'Noted,' said Graham. 'In the event of a Yeti invasion, seek out the nearest state ballroom.'

At the far end of the double-cube room, behind a podium on a raised stage, stood a thin man with a wave of shining golden hair. He looked like a struck match. Raising a small hammer in one hand, he lowered his mouth to a microphone.

'Sold!' he said, slamming down the hammer. It cracked against the podium like a gunshot.

Graham jumped.

The man gestured to an easel standing next to him on the stage, upon which sat an oil painting in an ornate frame. He turned to the audience and his golden wave of hair moved to point like a finger. 'Sold to the handsome industrialist in the good half of the Rich List.'

The man in question accepted the hooting congratulations of the other guests at his table.

Graham noticed that he was holding a small paddle with the number three on it. Evidently, they had arrived at some sort of auction. As an assistant wheeled the painting offstage, four more manhandled the next item on.

'And now we come to our final lot. Certainly the most unusual item to feature tonight. You'd better have a big entrance hall for this one – but of course you do.'

A tinkle of knowing laughter rose from the audience.

The item was shrouded beneath a white sheet but, judging from its outline, the object was roughly person-shaped, though taller and wider.

The Doctor produced her second alien device of the evening, a gently curved silver talon that sat snugly across her palm. Its mostly metal body was interlaced with a lava-coloured mineral and set with a single crystal at one end, which glowed when the device was in use. She called it her sonic screwdriver. Graham had been present when she constructed the device, a potent combination of Sheffield steel and Gallifreyan tech. Wielded by the Doctor, it could analyse almost any substance, open almost any door, assemble almost any bookcase. She aimed it across the room at the object. A second later, the sonic chirped and the Doctor studied its findings on a narrow display.

'That's what we came for. The same technology that blew up on the TARDIS is under that sheet.'

At that moment the auctioneer tugged at the sheet and it floated to the floor. There was a gasp from the audience as the object was revealed.

'It's a giant Oscar statue,' said Ryan.

'That's no Oscar,' said Yaz. 'It's a whatchamacallit. Y'know, story about that bull-thing killed by the guy who goes into the maze with the thread so he can find his way out again.'

'Minotaur,' said Graham.

The statue was the colour of molten bronze, its hulking body that of a muscle-bound man, but with the bluff head of a bull, from which sprung horns like handlebars.

'Looks like a Nimon to me,' said the Doctor.

Yaz had come to recognise the Doctor's differing tones of voice. There was regular concern followed by deep unease, and then a level of fear that caused her to make light-hearted jokes. Thankfully, she didn't seem to be at the most extreme level. Yet.

'An alien race, possibly the origin of your Minotaur myth. Romana and I came across them once.'

'I thought the Minotaur was Greek, not Roman,' said Graham.

'*Romana*,' the Doctor repeated, her gaze drifting off. 'Old friend.' She brightened. 'My canine companion was with us back then. Like your cop show, Yaz.'

Yaz blushed, as Ryan and Graham exchanged baffled looks.

'A rare example of what is believed to be a Minoan temple guard,' declared the auctioneer. 'Recently recovered from the depths of the Aegean Sea, and in quite remarkable condition. One of only two in the world, the other held in the private collection of Panos and Penelope Polichroniadis. Who will start me at half a million pounds?'

There was a momentary hush of expectation, and then at the table directly in front of the auctioneer a hand went up holding a small paddle sporting the number one.

Half a million! Graham looked around the room, wondering who could be foolish enough to outbid that kind of money.

'One million pounds!' sang out the Doctor.

4. Emergency Order Six-Three-Three Bravo Two-Zero Broadsword

Graham blinked. 'Doc?'

The auctioneer smiled. 'The bid is with the lady in the startlingly attractive jumpsuit.'

'What are you doing?' hissed Yaz.

'That thing may have been submerged for over two thousand years,' the Doctor said, inspecting the display on her sonic once more. 'But it's sucked down enough power to turn itself back on. Levels are low for now, but they're building. We have to assume that at some point it'll go off like the one on the TARDIS. And, when it does, it'll take London with it, along with most of the southeast. We must get it out of here, and there's only one way to do that.' She called out, 'Two million pounds!'

'Doc,' said Graham. 'You're bidding against yourself.'

She shrugged. 'It's only money.'

The paddle with the number one went up again, along with the bid. The Doctor matched it. Sensing this private game was about to turn oligarchically expensive, the other members of the audience left the two bidders to fight it out. In less than a minute, the sum had reached three and a half million. Ryan was grinning with a kind of mad exhilaration, but Yaz was open-mouthed and Graham felt faint.

The competing bidder gabbled into his mobile phone, sweat pouring off his brow. Across the back of the handset, Graham noticed a logo he didn't recognise: a sideways figure eight, and beneath it, etched in gold, the word *Aénaos*. As he registered it, he realised that every person across the room possessed the same handset.

The Doctor had noticed too. '*Aénaos*. The Greek word for perpetual, and the symbol means the same,' she noted. 'Interesting. I haven't seen this much Greek influence since that birthday lunch with Socrates, Aristotle and Plato. Which reminds me, Aristotle still owes me for the party hats.' The Doctor raised her hand and called out, 'Four million pounds.'

There were gasps from the audience, and this time no automatic increase from the opposing side.

Graham surmised what was going on: the man had orders to secure the statue for whoever was on the other end of that call, but thanks to the Doctor's meddling he was failing in his task. 'He's not the bidder,' Graham muttered. 'Someone else wants that statue.'

'Just what I was thinking,' said the Doctor, fiddling with the settings on her sonic and firing a discreet blast in the man's direction. Graham saw the immediate effect, as the man's face screwed up and he glared accusingly at his phone. Desperately, he attempted to redial, but the Doctor had cut him off. The bidding had already gone way higher than anyone expected and, without permission to increase his bid further, he could only watch in dismay as the auctioneer lowered the gavel.

BANG!

'Sold!'

The auctioneer smoothed his hair and regarded the curious group standing in front of him. The blonde woman was the winning bidder of the final item in the auction, the other three presumably her entourage. In his experience, the super-rich always travelled with their 'people', who invariably included an assistant, often two, and at least one bodyguard. The second woman looked like she could handle herself in a fight, which would make the young man the personal assistant. As for the older man, he was the odd one out. A driver, perhaps? But the drivers always stayed put in the limo. The auctioneer had checked and none of them was on the official guest list, but he could make an exception for anyone who'd just spent four million pounds. Following the concluding bid, the bronze of the Minotaur had been wheeled off in preparation for its dispatch.

'We will, of course, organise for your item to be shipped to any of your residences across the world. If you could just specify where –'

'We'll take it to go,' said the blonde woman. 'No need to wrap it.' She held a sheet of paper up to the auctioneer's face. 'Cashier's cheque from the Bank of Karabraxos?'

For a split second, the auctioneer was sure the paper was blank, but he blinked and the sheet filled with detail. He hadn't heard of the bank but was perfectly used to dealing with obscure offshore accounts. It certainly appeared to be a cashier's cheque, filled out to the right amount. And what a fabulous amount it was!

As he went to take the cheque, out of the corner of his eye he saw one of the auction assistants come running up. She cupped a hand to whisper in his ear. Upon hearing the news, he felt his mane of hair wilt.

'What do you mean, *gone*?'

The assistant confirmed the news.

Twitching with apologies, the auctioneer turned back to the winning bidder. 'I'm terribly sorry, but we seem to have . . . um . . . *mislaid* your item.'

'Mislaid it?' protested the driver. 'We're not talking about a set of car keys!'

'I'm sure it will . . . turn up.' He coughed, still reaching for the cheque. 'Again, my profuse apologies.'

The driver snapped the cheque out of his grasp.

The bodyguard pulled her charge aside and whispered, 'Doctor, do you think it walked off?'

Used to listening for bids across large auction rooms, the auctioneer picked up the whispered question. *Walked off?* What on Earth was she talking about?

'Possibly, but unlikely,' replied the woman he now knew to be a doctor. 'If it's some kind of robot, its power levels are still too low for autonomous movement. But give it an hour . . .'

Now they were talking about robots. This had to be some kind of prank. What kind of doctor *was* this woman?

'Then that guy took it,' said the personal assistant. 'The bloke you were bidding against.'

'Good shout, Ryan.' The Doctor spun round to face the auctioneer. 'The other bidder – what's his name?'

Finally, the auctioneer was back on solid ground. He clasped his hands together. 'I regret that data-protection laws do not permit me –'

The bodyguard took a step towards him. 'You just lost our four-million-pound statue. A suspicious person might imagine there was some kind of illegal activity going on here.'

He began to object, but only got so far as opening his mouth before she pressed on.

'A conviction of handling stolen property wouldn't look good for a reputable auctioneer such as yourself.'

He gawped. Felt a dryness in his throat. It was true that the owner of the statue had been somewhat *vague* regarding its origins, but . . .

The bodyguard pushed her face into his. 'I suggest you come up with a name and fa–'

'He is an agent for the Polichroniadis family,' the auctioneer blurted, scribbling down an address in nearby Knightsbridge.

'Thanks!' The Doctor snatched the address from him and set off, followed by her entourage. He watched them leave. Something inside was yelling at him that he had just experienced one of the most important encounters of his life.

'Robot?' he ventured weakly after the departing Doctor.

She waved the paper without looking back. 'Nothing to worry about. Your planet's safety is in the hands of the professionals.' With that, she flung open a door and marched through it. The others trooped after her.

A second or two later, the four reappeared, the Doctor leading the way with the same confident strut.

'And that, of course, is a storeroom,' she declared, marching towards the actual exit.

They left the banqueting hall and were quickly back out on the pavement. 'It's a couple of miles from here,' said the Doctor, reading the address. She hummed and hawed. 'In London traffic at this time, I reckon about six hours by cab.'

'TARDIS?' Yaz suggested.

The Doctor pulled a face. 'We could well end up in Knightsbridge, but I wouldn't bet on it being this century.'

'Follow me,' said Graham with a purposeful air. 'I know the fastest way.'

Ignoring the stream of black cabs whizzing up and down the wide road, he promptly led them to a bus stop that was nearby. Almost immediately a red double-decker with the number thirteen on the destination board trundled to a halt. The hydraulic doors hissed open and Graham began to board.

'You want to take the bus?' said Yaz, not attempting to hide her doubt.

Ryan was consulting the route map at the stop. 'The thirteen goes in the opposite direction of where we want to be.'

'Trust me,' said Graham.

'You heard the man,' said the Doctor, ushering them into the belly of the bus like schoolchildren on a class trip.

Graham paused next to the driver's compartment, which was separated from the main section by a Plexiglas window. He rapped on it to attract the driver's attention.

'I am driver Graham O'Brien of the Stagecoach Sheffield squadron, and I hereby invoke

43

Emergency Order Six-Three-Three Bravo Two-Zero Broadsword.'

At the mention of the phrase, the driver's eyes widened and he gave a shocked nod. Grabbing a handset from his dashboard, he broadcast an urgent announcement requesting that all passengers disembark immediately, owing to a potentially dangerous fuel leak. Grumbling, but wary of the hazard, they complied smartly.

'There's a fuel leak?' Ryan looked alarmed.

'No,' Graham whispered, forcing a smile for the benefit of the leaving passengers. 'It's the secret code of the bus-driving fraternity. Only to be used in a national emergency.' Before joining the Doctor, Graham had spent a considerable portion of his life sitting at the wheel of a bus just like this one. He turned back to the driver and gave him the Knightsbridge address, saying, 'We're going in fast and we're not stopping for anything. I need maximum cover.'

The driver adjusted a setting on the dashboard and keyed his mic once again. 'This is Red Thirteen to all drivers in the vicinity. A national emergency order has been triggered and verified. Prepare to initiate Strike Pattern Alpha.'

Over the airwaves came a series of acknowledgements.

'Red Sixty-six, standing by.'

'Red Ninety-seven, standing by.'

'Red Five, standing by.'

Several more buses reported their readiness, and the driver of the number thirteen issued a final command. 'Lock hydraulic doors in attack position.'

The bus doors hissed shut as the last passenger disembarked.

Graham grabbed the pole anchored between the floor and ceiling. 'Hold on to something,' he ordered the others. 'This could get rough.'

The bus lurched away from the stop, slewing round a hundred and eighty degrees and crossing several lanes of surprised traffic, before muscling along the busy road. When they reached the next junction, they found the cross-traffic blocked on both sides by two more buses, which had positioned themselves across the road, allowing the number thirteen to press on without pausing. The same helpful tactic continued along their route. Buses held back cars and cabs and livid white vans, permitting the number thirteen to punch a hole through what would otherwise have been impenetrable traffic. All the while, Graham stood tall at the front of the bus, gazing down the road and gripping the pole like Moses with his staff contemplating the Red Sea.

The bus deposited them outside a mansion house opposite a leafy garden square. The house was set back from the road, half hidden behind a black wrought-iron fence and a hedge so neat it looked as though it had been shaped with a laser-guided trimmer. Judging by the array of cameras and the discreet pulse of light at every window, the owners had spent an unfeasible amount of money on an advanced security system. It took the Doctor exactly four seconds to subdue the detectors and disable the cameras, and a further eight to open the gate and the reinforced front door.

She and the others found themselves standing in a grand entrance hall. The lights were on, but nobody was home.

Ryan had never been in a house like this. He'd seen them from the outside, but now it struck him that he'd visited more alien planets than grand mansions. The hall had a black-and-white floor like a chessboard, a curving staircase, lots of gold and marble, and huge oil paintings hanging on the walls. Several corridors branched off the entrance hall.

'Which way?' said Yaz.

The Doctor adjusted her sonic. 'Bronze is an alloy, which means it's made of a combination of copper and another metal, like nickel or zinc.

In the past, people would use whatever was lying around – cooking pots, old swords, that kind of thing. Which is good for us, as it means our Minotaur friend gives off a unique signature. One I can tune in to using my sonic screwdriver.' The sonic began to bleep faintly. 'Sort of a Findotaur.' She swung the device round in an attempt to lock on to the signal. Left, right, up –

   'Down!'

5. Penelope

They strode along wood-panelled corridors filled with paintings that seemed vaguely familiar to Ryan. He was pretty sure he remembered seeing that one with the water lilies on a school trip to the art gallery.

'That auctioneer said this place belongs to the Polichroniadis family. What do you know about them?' asked the Doctor.

'Never heard of them,' said Yaz, and the other two agreed.

'Curious,' said the Doctor. 'You Earthlings make celebrities out of your super-rich, so it's a fair bet that one of you should know their name. Especially a name as memorable as theirs. And, if they weren't famous ten years ago when we first met, that suggests they got rich enough in that brief time to afford a place like this and fill it with Impressionists.'

'Maybe they won the lottery,' Ryan suggested.

'Maybe,' echoed the Doctor, but Ryan could tell she was working on another hypothesis. One she wasn't yet willing to share.

'D'you think they're aliens with a complicated plot to take over the world?' asked Graham. 'Hiding behind their money and the cloak of respectability?'

'Funny how often that turns out to be the case, isn't it?' mused the Doctor.

The sonic trail led to a glass lift, which they took down to the lowest of three sublevels, first passing through a floor containing a swimming pool.

'Looks bigger than yours, Doc,' Graham gently ribbed her.

Ryan let out a long whistle as they reached the next level: an underground parking garage. Ferraris and Bugattis basked like movie stars, spotlights jostling to highlight the sheen of their perfectly polished bodies. You didn't have to have Ryan's passion for motors to appreciate the automotive art in there.

The lift came to a smooth stop at the third and final level. It was a private museum filled with yet more works of art. They stepped out of the lift, and passed through the first gallery in silence. Apart from the discreet hum of the air-conditioning units that kept the gallery at the ideal temperature and humidity, the only sound was the chirping of the Doctor's 'Findotaur'. Judging by its increased rhythm, they were drawing closer to their goal. The Doctor paused briefly next to one of the paintings.

'Da Vinci's "Leda and the Swan",' she said, peering fascinatedly at the picture. 'Missing for over three hundred years. I must let him know it's in one piece.'

A scream pierced the air.

'Through there,' said Yaz, making swiftly for an arched doorway that led to the next gallery.

The circular chamber was a forest of bronze statues illuminated by soft light that fell from recessed spots in the ceiling. Classical figures of men, women and animals occupied plinths, variously readying to throw a spear or be speared, raising a sword or embracing a lover.

'Look,' hissed Graham, pointing a trembling finger.

On the far side of the room stood the Minotaur. At its cloven feet lay the unmoving body of the man who'd bid against them at the auction, face down on the mosaic floor.

Ignoring the cautionary cries of the others, Yaz rushed to the man's side and carefully turned his body over. His neck was at an odd angle and his eyes stared out blankly. One side of his face was scarred where a powerful blow had landed. Even as she felt for a pulse, she knew it was hopeless.

'Poor man,' said the Doctor, as Yaz gently closed his eyelids.

Graham approached, keeping a close watch on the looming bronze. 'D'you think *it* did this?' he asked.

'Definitely not.' The sonic bleeped softly and the Doctor raised a puzzled eyebrow. 'This is not our Minotaur. It's giving off a different signature.'

'Didn't the auctioneer say there were two?' said Ryan. 'And the other was in the private collection of the Poly-whatsits? This must be it.'

'So, where's ours?' said Yaz.

A waft of stale air briefly overpowered the artificially freshened stuff that the museum system pumped through the gallery. It drifted out of another archway that led into darkness. As the Doctor turned the sonic towards it, the device gave off an insistent tone.

'Not good,' she said.

'Don't say that,' pleaded Graham.

51

'I'd say, from this, our Minotaur has acquired enough power for self-propulsion. It's on the move.'

Ryan had been travelling with the Doctor and the others for – how long was it now? Time was, ironically enough, one of the trickier things to keep track of when you were in the Doctor's company. Until the moment he'd joined her, his life had been boringly chronological: one day after the other, in the same predictable order. Now, however, a typical week went something like Monday, Tuesday, Giant Bronze Walking Statue.

There was a low groan from nearby, and for one odd moment Ryan imagined it had come from a statue of a woman holding an urn and a bunch of grapes. Then he saw a head of tight black curls poking out from behind the base of the statue. He hurried over.

There lay a young woman, her eyes wide and staring. She groaned again. She was dazed, but at least she was alive. A livid cut striped her forehead and, as she sat up, blood trickled down her olive skin and between a pair of large round eyes a startling violet colour. As they focused on Ryan, they seemed to him to shine with mistrust.

'Ryan, stay with her,' ordered the Doctor, already swinging round to march off through the archway. 'We have to find that thing – and quickly.'

Yaz went after the Doctor, while Graham hesitated, torn between following or remaining behind to help his grandson.

'Go,' said Ryan. 'I can look after things here.'

Graham nodded and dashed after the others, the sound of their footsteps receding quickly into the gloom.

'I can look after myself,' objected the woman, attempting to stand. Despite her claim, as soon as she got to her feet she stumbled.

Ryan caught her in his arms, preventing her from crashing down against the hard mosaic floor.

'Get off me!' she said, pushing him away. 'I'm calling the police.'

'Fine.' Ryan folded his arms. 'And, when they get here, I'm sure they'll be interested to find a dead body and hear all about our stolen statue.'

He held the woman's fierce gaze. Clearly unhappy about having to back down in the face of his threat, she resorted to another tack.

'What are you doing in my house?'

For the first time, Ryan registered that she spoke perfect English, but with an accent he couldn't place. The TARDIS had this weird influence field, which meant that, so long as it was in range, you could understand everything that was said to you by any alien race, and vice versa. So, even if he was talking to aliens with four tongues and a language consisting of ultrasonic squawks, to him they would seem to be speaking English. Half the time they sounded like they were from Yorkshire. Yet another of the TARDIS's little jokes.

And then it struck him. '*Your* house? Then you're . . .' He aimed for the high bar of her name. 'Poli . . . um . . . thingy.' And missed.

'*Poli-chroni-adis*,' she said irritably, pronouncing it with exaggerated care. 'Penelope Polichroniadis. Why can no one in this cold country say my name properly?' Her expression darkened. 'You still haven't answered my question. Why are you and your colleagues here? Are you robbing me?' She raised an eyebrow as if the prospect amused her.

'God, no!' said Ryan. 'We're not burglars, we're . . .' He hesitated, unsure where to start. Explanations involving the Doctor invariably required a long run-up. He tailed off, seeing that Penelope had lost interest and was barely listening. Instead, she was gazing into his eyes. No, not both eyes – just one of them. Gently she reached out and gripped his head in her hands, angling it so that the light shone directly in his face.

'Fascinating,' she said. 'Save your explanation for my brother.'

Unlike the art gallery, with its pitch-perfect lighting and controlled humidity, this place was still more subterranean cave than billionaire's basement conversion. *Not easy to traverse in a ballgown*, Yaz thought, hitching up the silver dress with one hand while holding her phone in the other, its torch lighting their way across the rough earthen floor. She'd ditched the heels back at the entrance and could feel the cold soil through the soles of her stockinged feet.

She, Graham and the Doctor were following a series of hoofed impressions. The darkness hugged them, barely troubled by the prick of light; it was a darkness that had slept for centuries, deep beneath the comings and goings of human-kind, and it would take more than a weedy flash on the back of a smartphone to bother it. Up ahead, Yaz could just make out the dim shape of the Doctor, the amber light from her pulsing sonic tracing a faint outline round her body. The Doctor never broke stride, Yaz thought. Not even when pursuing a nine-foot-tall bronze killing machine with a nuclear bomb for a heart. It was either foolhardy confidence beyond human understanding or . . . No, it was definitely that.

At last, they came to the far side of the cave. The hoofprints stopped at a freshly dug hole where the rock wall met the soil. Chunks of stone and great lumps of dirt lay strewn about the ground. The Minotaur had torn through the rock with its bare hooves.

'Big enough for our friend to squeeze through – horns turned to the side, obviously,' said the Doctor, grasping the edges of the hole and preparing to launch herself through it.

Graham laid a hand on her arm. 'What's the plan if we catch that thing?'

'It's a walking bomb,' said the Doctor. 'We defuse it.'

'What if it doesn't want to be defused?'

'Graham's got a point,' Yaz chimed in. 'To defuse a bomb, the first thing you need to know is what you're dealing with.'

'Did you do a course?' The Doctor wagged a knowing finger. 'You did, didn't you? Good for you, Yaz.'

Yaz ignored her. 'We don't know anything about this Minotaur. We need technical specifications . . . something.'

'There's an old Sontaran saying,' said the Doctor. 'For every probic vent there is a thumb just the right size.'

Yaz glimpsed Graham's puzzled expression and knew that it matched her own.

'No?' said the Doctor with a conceding shrug. 'Doesn't translate terribly well.'

'You're saying that the solution will be obvious when we catch the thing?' guessed Yaz.

'Exactly.' The Doctor turned to go, then paused. 'Well, probably not *obvious*. But I'll definitely figure out the answer before it goes *bang*.'

Yaz experienced a spike of anxiety. The Doctor's breezy confidence was a sure sign that she was worried about the outcome of their current adventure.

They clambered through the hole to emerge into more gloom. Yaz pointed the light down at her feet. The ground was no longer soil, but smooth concrete. Beyond that, she could see little more of their surroundings.

'I'm detecting a power source,' said the Doctor, reviewing the display on her sonic.

'Minotaur?' whispered Graham.

'Something else. Whatever it is hasn't been in use for a long time, but I think I can give it a temporary boost.' She extended the sonic and depressed one of its buttons. From nearby came a crackle of electricity and a shower of sparks, and a moment later the place was flooded with light. Yaz was momentarily dazzled by the sudden brightness. Her vision settled quickly.

They were on the platform of a London Underground station. Dust coated the tiled walls and lay thickly across the floor. It hung in the air too – recently disturbed, Yaz had no doubt, by the passing of the Minotaur. She scanned the platform for signs of its presence.

'Brompton Road,' Graham read from a sign on the wall. 'It's a ghost station.'

'Disused,' clarified the Doctor, seeing Yaz's puzzled expression.

'There are a number of them across the network,' said Graham. 'Some of them fell out of use, others were used during the Second World War as shelters. First time I've been in one.'

Yaz picked up the trail: a series of hoofprints led to the edge of the platform and disappeared. She felt a creep of unease as she peered down the dusty track into the wide mouth of the tunnel. The station may no longer have been in use, but it was still part of the Tube network. In her mind, that could mean only one thing.

'There's a Minotaur loose in the London Underground.'

6. Release the Mecha-Hounds

The boy clutched the precious bag tight to his chest. He smiled up at Dad, who was sitting next to him in the crowded carriage. They'd travelled into London together – just the two of them – on a special trip to spend his birthday money, and now they were on their way back home. The Tube train rattled and squealed as it plunged through the tunnel, heading west, and the boy thought back on the day. It had started badly. When they'd reached the big toy shop on Regent Street, he'd discovered to his dismay that his birthday money didn't quite stretch to the special-edition Transformer he'd been wishing for. He'd tried not to look disappointed.

'It's okay,' Dad had said, then paid the difference, advising him with a conspiratorial smile not to tell his little sister.

Now, after the excitement of the gift, the burger and the walk through busy central London, he was sleepy and looking forward to getting home. A yawn overtook him and he pressed himself into his dad's side. Lulled by the swaying motion of the train and the comforting pressure of the arm round his shoulder, he felt himself beginning to nod off.

The train lights flickered and died.

In the semi-darkness of the carriage, he glimpsed something out of the corner of one eye. It was outside the window. A shining face from a nightmare, with blazing eyes and great, curving horns.

The lights stuttered back on again, banishing the shadows, and it was gone.

'Torrin, what's up?' His dad gazed down at him in concern.

The boy's throat was constricted with fear. He couldn't speak. Even if he'd had the words, he wasn't sure what he would have said.

The carriage lurched sideways, causing the standing passengers to be thrown to the floor.

There was a complaining shriek of metal wheels on track and a sudden deceleration that snatched Torrin out of his dad's arms, hurling him into the aisle. He fell to the floor, spilling his precious toy from its bag. From the far end of the carriage came the crash of breaking glass, and then the screaming began.

The overhead lights flickered and buzzed like the wings of a trapped insect, strobing across the carriage and the terrified faces of the other passengers, which were all turned in the same direction. And then he saw it again – the face at the window. But it was inside now. A bronze monster, broad as a bull. With a snort, it charged down the aisle, tossing passengers aside. There was the crunch of breaking bones as soft bodies crashed into the compartment walls. The beast's horns scraped the ceiling, leaving two long gouges as it hurtled down the carriage towards Torrin. His new toy lay directly in its path. Not thinking, he dived headlong for it, and heard Dad scream his name. Fingers outstretched, he grasped the plastic Bumblebee and whipped it away, just as one great, shining hoof stamped down where a moment ago the toy had lain.

The monster paused, tilted its great head down to regard him with those hideous eyes. In the midst of the screams, Torrin felt immense heat roll off it – and something else too. It ticked like a bomb. He thrust out the Transformer, brandishing it before him like a weapon. The monster angled its huge head, scrutinising the tiny figure. And then it turned away. With a low, terrible cry that made Torrin shiver to his bones, it crashed straight through the carriage, tearing the wall apart as if it was made of paper, and bounded back out into the underground tunnel.

Dad's arms again, this time wrapped round him so tight he wondered if they'd ever let go. And Dad saying his name, over and over.

Ryan was reluctant to leave the dead man.

'He will be taken care of,' replied Penelope. 'I promise.'

There was a confidence in her tone that suggested to Ryan that Penelope was used to things being taken care of for her. Partially reassured, he followed her out of the museum, retracing his steps through the galleries. As they made their way through the house, he was aware of an unexpected sensation coursing through his body. It was probably all the adrenaline from the recent excitement, but rarely had he felt so full of energy. The two of them returned to the lift, and soon it had whisked them to the upper reaches of the mansion.

'Wait here,' Penelope commanded, leaving him alone in a long corridor outside a set of ornate double doors. She disappeared through them, and as she did Ryan caught a glimpse of the room beyond. The strange sight was enough to tempt him to risk another peek. He carefully cracked open one of the doors and pressed his eye to the gap.

On first sight, it appeared to be a regular if rather ostentatious bedroom, with an imposing four-poster bed against one wall and a large armoire opposite. However, between the two was something completely unexpected.

Ryan could only describe it as a gold sarcophagus.

It was about the length of a tall man, shaped to follow the contours of a human body and constructed from a substance that, if not real gold, gave off the precious metal's rich glow. Flanking it sat two of the strangest creatures he had ever seen, each with four legs supporting a flat, slab-like body. At first, Ryan thought they were some kind of weird bedside tables but, as Penelope crossed the floor towards the sarcophagus, they sat up like dogs. Mechanical dogs. They were headless and eyeless, but it was the way they moved that was most unnerving. With a whine of actuators and the puff of hydraulics,

63

the dog at the feet of the sarcophagus lifted itself up, its legs articulating at various joints as it began to move. There was something spider-like about the way it scuttled across the room. Only at the last second did Ryan realise that it was heading for the door through which he was spying.

'Oh no.'

Balancing on three legs, it extended the fourth, reaching up to tip the door handle. The door swung open and Ryan was exposed. The dog emitted a low rumbling sound that made Ryan's chest vibrate. It squatted back on its haunches, preparing to leap.

Ryan froze, at once intimidated by the dog's aggressive stance and fascinated by what made it tick. One day, he thought, his engineering-obsessed mind was going to get him hurt – or worse.

'Nice doggie.' Ryan peered at the assemblage. The slab of its body appeared to be a protective framework containing a motor and what he assumed to be a range of sensors.

'Scylla, no!'

The dog reacted to Penelope's command and, with a descending whine of power, switched instantly from attack mode to a passive state.

'I told you to wait outside.' Penelope glared at Ryan, but he barely heard her, his attention distracted by what was happening in the centre of the room.

The lid of the sarcophagus was opening.

Slowly, it hinged up along one side. A white gas seeped over the rim, and Ryan was aware of a sudden chill in the air. It had to be the gas – some kind of coolant, which meant the sarcophagus must be a sort of fridge. From inside, a pale hand reached up and gripped one edge. Ryan half expected Dracula to haul himself out, but instead of the Prince of Darkness it was an ordinary man who emerged. He had a boyish, handsome face from which gazed a pair of unblinking eyes the same startling colour as Penelope's. A head of sleek dark hair was gathered in a topknot. He stood up, stretched his arms, inhaled deeply and sprang lightly over the side, landing next to Penelope. Apart from a pair of shorts, he was naked, his skin puckered with the cold, though he didn't seem to register any discomfort. Penelope handed him a robe, which he wrapped himself in. She whispered something to him and he registered momentary surprise. As he tied the cord round his waist, he fixed his gaze on Ryan across the room.

'I'm Panos Polichroniadis,' he said, flashing a megawatt smile. 'I understand you've mislaid my Minotaur.'

7. The Sword of Aegeus

They'd lost the beast's trail on the Piccadilly Line. For once, the Doctor had chosen not to plunge on headlong, but instead regroup back at the mansion. Graham had the strong sense that she was brewing some fresh plan.

Ryan was waiting for them when they returned to the statue gallery. And he was not alone. Next to him was the young woman Graham had last seen lying injured on the floor, her wound now bandaged, and alongside her stood a young man with whom she shared a strong resemblance. They looked as if they'd been brought up beside a swimming pool, thought Graham, probably under southern European skies. The two displayed the healthy sheen that came from a lifelong diet of sun-ripened tomatoes and non-fried fish. It crossed his mind, with no small measure of annoyance, that wherever they went in time and space everyone they met was invariably youthful and good-looking. Was that statistically likely? He wondered whether, as well as its translation field, the TARDIS might also exert a 'handsome' field.

At the man's heels trotted a strange pair of frankly terrifying mechanical dog-spider things. They came to sniff at the Doctor and the others, long metal legs clacking on the floor, sensors humming. One of the monstrosities padded close enough for Graham to hear, above the click of its claws, a faint ticking rising from its mechanism. With a shiver, he realised that it reminded him of the Minotaur.

'Hello, I'm the Doctor.' She bounded up to the man and woman. 'I'm here to help.'

'You can start by helping us understand why you broke in to our house,' the woman retorted.

Graham watched as Ryan interposed himself. 'Uh, Doctor, this is Penelope and Panos *Poli-chroni-adis*,' he said, pronouncing the word with great deliberation. Having successfully negotiated the tripwire of their surname, he turned to Penelope with a hopeful smile.

'Or,' said Yaz, 'we could start with you explaining why your agent stole our statue from the auction. And how he ended up dead.'

'An honest mistake,' said Panos. 'When his phone malfunctioned, Alexander was unable to contact Penelope for instructions. He panicked.'

'As soon as he returned with the statue,' Penelope went on, 'I realised what he had done. I was in the process of contacting the auction house when the statue –' she hesitated, as if she couldn't quite believe what she was saying – 'came alive. It killed poor Alexander, and injured me.'

'Not alive,' corrected the Doctor. 'It's a machine powered by a remarkable engine.'

At the mention of the engine, Graham noticed a glance pass between brother and sister. He didn't trust either of them. People with nothing to hide didn't own robot attack pets. Those things were giving him the heebie-jeebies.

'Unfortunately, Alexander might not be its last victim,' the Doctor went on. 'The engine is highly unstable. Your statue is a walking bomb.'

'You seem to know a lot about it, Doctor,' said Penelope.

'Let's just say this is not my first Minotaur rodeo.'

The atmosphere in the room had altered, the earlier dissent now replaced by a truce that verged on collaboration. Graham noted that one of the Doctor's greatest roles was as a peacemaker.

'So how do we stop it?' asked Panos.

Yaz stood in the shadow of the other Minotaur statue. 'How did you make this one safe?'

'Good thinking, Yaz,' said the Doctor. 'If we know that, then we can apply the same technique to our rogue.'

But Yaz's question puzzled the Polichroniadis siblings. 'There was no need to make it safe,' said Penelope.

'The statue was inert when we acquired it,' explained Panos.

'The two statues are different,' said the Doctor, examining the exterior of the one in front of her. 'The bronze of this one is pitted and displays a sickly green hue. The metal has "oxidised", which means that it's been exposed to air.'

'Not just air,' Panos continued. 'When this statue was reclaimed from the bottom of the Aegean Sea, it was evident that the internal workings had been ravaged by saltwater over the course of thousands of years. No amount of my tinkering could return it to working order.'

'*Your* tinkering?' said the Doctor.

'My brother is a watchmaker,' said Penelope proudly.

'Hardly,' he demurred. 'Once upon a time, I repaired watches and clocks in the family business on Crete. But that was a lifetime ago.'

'How does a simple watch repairman from the Greek islands end up in a house like this?' asked Yaz.

'Good fortune,' Panos replied obliquely, his mouth crinkling in a roguish smile.

'Lucky you didn't get it going again,' said the Doctor. 'It'd probably have killed you. Your statue and the one we're looking for were built by a mysterious civilisation known as the Minoans. From what I've been able to tell from my sonic scans, the exterior skin is an unusually tough bronze alloy, the horns and claws are diamond-tipped, and inside the body is a formidably strong skeleton with an engine containing a surprising clockwork element. The engine draws its power from an as yet unidentified source, and the whole creature is designed to be an unstoppable killing machine.'

Even in the face of this terrifying description, Ryan couldn't help but be impressed. 'A clockwork Terminator. Cool.'

'Hang about,' said Graham. 'If they were both dunked in the sea for thousands of years, how come the missing Minotaur isn't in the same state as this one?'

'Unlike this one, our runaway was found perfectly sealed in a bronze casket.'

'I'm curious,' said Yaz, clearly wishing to continue her line of questioning. 'Why did you want the statue in the first place?'

Panos met her inquisitive gaze with a brazen stare, then hooked a finger, beckoning her to follow.

They trooped after him into another gallery, one they had missed on their way through the first time. It was the largest of the rooms in the subterranean museum and was packed with exhibits. Elaborate gold jewellery shone from glass cases: necklaces, bracelets and pins shaped into the likenesses of birds, fish and insects. A golden bee looked real enough to sting. There were row upon row of ceramic urns and jugs decorated with simple but stunning geometric designs. Cups in gold and bronze filled yet more displays, and one entire wall was a vivid fresco depicting a leaping bull. The ancient civilisation's military story was also told here, in the form of bronze helmets, swords and spears. They were grouped around a glass cabinet set beneath a pool of light, containing a single sword, presumably of greater historical importance than the rest.

Panos gestured around the room. 'I am the world's foremost collector of Minoan antiquities.

The Cretan Bull was to take pride of place.' A space had been made for the statue in the centre of the room. He theatrically placed a hand on his heart. 'Truly, I had no idea of the terrible threat it contained.' Panos bowed his head in the affectation of an apology.

Graham didn't believe that for a second.

'If you're the expert,' said Ryan, 'then do you have any idea how we stop that thing?'

'I regret not,' said Panos. 'I am but a humble collector.'

'I think I know how,' said the Doctor, her eyes shining. 'We're going old school.' She looked around the room. 'For five points, who's the last person to have successfully defeated a Minotaur?'

'Harry Hamlin,' replied Graham. '*Clash of the Titans*. Great film.'

'I believe he played the role of Perseus,' corrected Penelope. 'Who, according to myth, overcame the gorgon Medusa. It was Theseus who slew the Minotaur.'

'Yeah, sorry, Graham, she's dead right,' said the Doctor. 'Five points to Penelope.' She began walking the length of the military exhibit, her finger poised over various spears and swords as she passed them. 'The story goes that, following the usual god-and-mortal shenanigans, King

Minos instructed a chap called Daedalus, who was Icarus's dad –'

'The one who flew too close to the sun?' said Yaz.

'If you believe that sort of thing,' said the Doctor. 'Anyway, Daedalus built a labyrinth in Knossos, on the island of Crete, to hold the Minotaur. He offered it human sacrifices, sending young men and women into the maze to be eaten by the monster. A square-jawed, clean-limbed youth called Theseus decided to put an end to all the devouring. With the help of the king's daughter, Ariadne, they navigated the labyrinth, marking their route with a ball of golden thread so that they wouldn't get lost. At the heart of the maze, Theseus put paid to the Minotaur using his dad's sword.'

She paused next to the solitary sword in its own glass case. With a quick blast of her sonic screwdriver, the locked door opened.

Panos gasped. 'No, please!'

But it was too late. The Doctor reached in, clasped the hilt and drew it out of the display case.

'Everyone's heard about the golden thread, but few remember Theseus's trusty blade, the Sword of Aegeus.'

It was a short, stubby weapon the same dull green as the oxidised bronze statue. Edges once

73

sharp enough to slice through mythical monsters were now brittle with age and ragged as a crow's wings. Judging from the burnished scraps that clung to it, the hilt had at one time been gold-plated, but long ago lost its lustre. A teardrop crystal protruding from its base was as cloudy as a cataract-scarred eye.

'Please be careful, Doctor.' There was genuine apprehension in Panos's voice. 'That weapon is unique – and priceless.'

'Is it the real thing?' Ryan asked, incredulous. 'The Sword of Ages?'

'*Aegeus*,' corrected Panos. 'And no one can say with certainty.' Despite his concern for the welfare of the exhibit, he seemed energised by the question. 'But see the markings on the blade?'

Through the patina of age, what looked to Ryan like random scoring was visible along the length of the sword.

'It's known as Linear A, or Minoan, which is a writing system that, unfortunately, remains undeciphered to this day. However, I suspect that what is written here will establish its provenance.'

'Prove– what?' asked Ryan.

'Who owned it,' explained the Doctor, 'which usually tells you whether a work of art is authentic.'

Panos barrelled on, his enthusiasm almost overtaking his words. 'I am funding long-term linguistic research to that end, and in a decade or two hope to be able to prove that this is indeed the sword that slew the Minotaur.'

'It's not,' said the Doctor.

Panos looked as surprised and outraged as a man who had just run smack into a glass wall.

'Not exactly,' she conceded. 'For a start, it's not Minoan. It's Nimon – an alien language. And this isn't a weapon. The markings are a series of instructions, like a computer program. The sword is the delivery system. See, if I designed a robotic killer temple guard, I'd want to be able to program it to follow my commands, wouldn't I?'

'You're saying the sword can tell the Minotaur what to do?' said Yaz. 'How?'

'I noticed something on the statue in the other gallery,' replied the Doctor. 'A slot between its shoulder blades.' The Doctor held the sword level and, closing one eye, sighted along its length. 'Just the right size to fit this –' She thrust it forward.

Graham ducked out of the way with a complaining, 'Hey!'

'Think of it like an ancient Greek port. USB rather than Corfu.' The Doctor twirled the sword in one hand. 'Now all we have to do is insert this sword into our Minotaur.'

'That's *all*, is it?' Graham grumbled.

'But, Doctor,' said Yaz. 'How d'you know that the program will deactivate the Minotaur?'

The Doctor pointed to a combination of lines and circles. 'See here? The Nimon phrase for "come to an end".' She struck off, swinging the sword round her head. 'Once more unto the breach, dear friends. We have a computer to deactivate.' She paused. 'Doesn't sound as good as a monster to slay, does it?'

8. Ovid and Out

In all the excitement since the others had returned from their first foray into the tunnels, Ryan hadn't found an opportunity to tell them what he'd seen in the upstairs bedroom. Now, as they prepared to venture out again, he seized a moment alone with Yaz.

'A gold sarcophagus?' Yaz repeated, trying to understand.

'The inside was cold,' said Ryan. 'Like he was putting himself on ice. What d'you think was going on with that?'

Yaz gave a puzzled shrug. 'Might be some kind of super-rich person's beauty treatment.

Y'know, like those people who inject their own blood into their face to stay young.'

Ryan did not know. He wasn't good with needles and he paled at the thought of voluntarily sticking one in your own face, especially to inject yourself with blood. But Yaz's explanation was as good as any, so he gave it no more thought. And, anyway, there were bigger things to worry about.

They gathered in the statue gallery to plan out the mission. The inert Minotaur cast its long shadow across the mosaic floor as the Doctor paced up and down, laying out the strategy.

'First, we find our Minotaur, then we trap it so we can get close enough to insert the Sword of Aegeus into the port on its back.'

'I cannot possibly allow you to take the sword,' said Panos, and before the Doctor could offer an objection he grinned. '*I* shall be our Theseus.'

Penelope looked askance at her brother. 'You're not thinking of accompanying these lunatics, are you?'

Yaz bristled at the insult.

Panos brushed off his sister's concern. 'I feel the burden of responsibility. After all, if it weren't for my passion for Minoan art, that statue would almost certainly still be at the bottom of the Aegean Sea.'

There was a sonorous chime from his pocket and he pulled out a mobile phone. Graham noticed the same 'perpetual' logo he'd seen on the phones belonging to the people at the auction.

Panos checked the alert that had popped up. 'It seems our escapee has made the news.'

He flicked through a cascade of reports that had just appeared. Despite numerous eyewitness sightings, it seemed that most of the news outlets were wary of the story, couching it in terms that would allow them to walk back their reporting should the whole thing turn out to be a viral advertising campaign for jeans.

Graham didn't hide his exasperation. 'That sums up the modern world. A living giant bronze statue of a Greek myth shows up on the Piccadilly Line, and nobody believes it.'

'*That* sums it up?' Ryan shook his head.

'But it's good for us,' said Yaz. 'If people don't believe the Minotaur is a genuine threat, there's less likely to be a panic.'

The Doctor agreed. 'I tried something similar on Earth in 1938. Had a friend broadcast a radio play about a Martian invasion, called *War of the Worlds*. I was using it as a cover for a *real* Martian invasion by Ice Warriors.' She shrugged at the memory. 'Mind you, still caused a panic. Best-laid plans, eh?'

79

Panos lowered his phone. 'The Underground is a big place. Where do we start looking?'

'The Doctor has a way of tracking the Minotaur,' said Ryan.

'Unfortunately, it's not perfect,' said the Doctor. 'I need to be close enough to pick up the signal through the tunnels. I can't tell where the Minotaur is right now – not from here.'

'Check the news reports. Where was the latest sighting?' said Yaz. 'We should start the search from there.'

The Doctor had noticed a bookcase containing a series of volumes, faded red spines etched with gold print. 'Or we could check the *oldest* news report. Ovid's *Metamorphoses*,' she said, plucking a volume from midway through the series. 'Western literature's go-to guy for Classical myth since 8 AD.'

'And a dab hand at the pole vault,' added Graham.

The Doctor regarded him with a puzzled expression.

'You always do that. Mention some famous person from history, then drop in that you knew them by throwing in a random fact no one else could possibly know.' Graham looked around at the others to back him up. 'Come on. It's not just me.'

The Doctor threw him a dirty look and turned the brittle pages of the book. 'Ovid wrote about the Minotaur. Ever since I set eyes on that statue, it's been stuck in my head, like the lyrics to "Do You Want to Build a Snowman?" '

Graham threw up his hands. 'Great. Now they're going to be stuck in mine.'

'It seems our mechanical Minotaur was originally designed to patrol the labyrinth, and my guess is it's still following its programming. But, instead of the Minoan maze, it's set up shop in the closest thing to it: the Tube network. Ah, here it is,' she said, reading out the relevant section in the original Latin before Yaz interrupted. The Doctor paraphrased in English. 'The Minotaur is found *at the heart* of the labyrinth.'

Panos turned to his phone. 'I have a map of the Underground on here. We can identify the geographical centre of the network.'

'The heart of the labyrinth isn't its centre,' said the Doctor.

With the great book cradled in her arms Ryan thought she resembled a fire-and-brimstone preacher about to deliver a sermon. Panos stopped scrolling through his apps. The others fell quiet. Even the statues seemed to be listening.

'The labyrinth always leads down. Towards Hell. The Minotaur is a creature of the underworld.

It seeks out the darkness. Which means that we'll find it in the deepest, darkest part of the Underground.'

She closed the book, the covers coming together with a thunderous clap.

'Hampstead?' said Yaz. 'You're quite sure it's Hampstead Tube?'

They had arrived outside the station in North London, this time taking Panos's autonomous Bentley SUV to traverse the city rather than relying on Graham's unique bus pass. There had been a minor tussle over who got to sit up front. Ryan had called dibs, owing to his fascination for all things automotive. But the Doctor trumped him by saying she got carsick if she travelled in the back, so Ryan had found himself stuck in the middle seat between Graham and Yaz.

'She travels across time and space in a spinning police box,' he'd muttered crossly. 'Never seen her throw up once.'

A police cordon was already in place outside the station entrance, thanks to Panos. It had proved shockingly easy for him to call in a favour from a figure he referred to only as 'someone in authority'. One brief phone conversation and the station had been shut down. Panos refused to identify the mysterious person, but Yaz was pretty sure she'd glimpsed the mayor's number on his contacts list. As much as it irritated her to see such powerful influence in action, Yaz knew that having the Underground station to themselves was essential if they were going to successfully trap the Minotaur. Panos was currently charming the two police officers at the entrance.

The Doctor opened the car's capacious boot. The two mechanical dogs, Scylla and Charybdis, uncoiled themselves and sprang out on to the pavement like a couple of Labradors. Panos had insisted that they'd be useful in the hunt, though Graham muttered that he'd rather meet the Minotaur in a dark tunnel than one of those things.

'You might very well get your wish.' The Doctor smiled.

Once the dogs had vacated the boot, she reached in and removed the other equipment they'd need for the mission: the Sword of Aegeus, several torches and a large wooden spool wound with a coil of steel cable. 'Hampstead is the deepest station on the network,' said the Doctor. 'The platform is fifty-nine metres below street level.' She shoved the cable into Ryan's arms.

Panos beckoned to them with a thumbs-up.

83

'Time to brave the labyrinth,' said the Doctor, setting off after him.

She and the TARDIS crew passed by the police officers unnoticed; the officers' startled attention was fixed upon the mechanical dogs scuttling alongside. They might have paid more attention to Yaz if she'd still been wearing her silver dress, but she'd changed out of it into a pair of jeans and a jumper that Penelope had lent her. Ryan and Graham had changed too, in order to avoid attracting attention. The Doctor, as ever, stood out like an alien thumb.

The ticket hall was quiet, the barriers stuck open and the ticket office unmanned. Although empty, the office contained several active monitors, displaying video from cameras located down at the platform level and inside the north- and southbound tunnels.

'Graham, I want you to stay up here,' said the Doctor. He began to object, but she cut him off. 'We need someone to watch the monitors. You'll be our eyes.'

'You'll each need one of these to keep in touch,' said Panos, handing out mobile phones with the now-familiar Aénaos logo. 'They'll work with the Wi-Fi on the platforms, but once you're in the tunnels the signal will be patchy at best. I've set them up like a conference call – when one of us talks, all of us will be able to hear and respond.'

Ryan regarded the phone with delight. 'I was due an upgrade.'

'One more thing,' the Doctor said to Graham, fishing a key from a hook in the office. 'This will let you manually operate the lifts.' She led him to a panel next to the entrance and showed him how to operate the controls. 'When the time comes, I'll signal you to bring us up. Got it?'

He nodded and, with an anxious glance at his grandson, wished them luck as they filed into the lift.

The doors closed on the ticket hall. Yaz felt her stomach lurch as they began their descent. Utterly reliable electrical-hydraulic mechanisms unspooled them into the depths, like a shark cage plunging into the abyss. Less than thirty seconds later, they emerged into a short corridor of green-tiled walls. The air felt heavier down here, or perhaps it was the weight of anxiety. As they passed along the corridor, the only sound was the clicking of the mechanical dogs' claws on the floor. Yaz's torch flashed on a line of text – THERE'S NO ESCAPE! – and she then saw it was a strapline, splashed across a poster for the latest big-budget monster movie. It was one of a range of colourful posters advertising the latest books and films.

The corridor led to two platforms: one for northbound services, the other southbound, both silent and empty. From somewhere in the distance came the rumble of a Tube train. Although this stretch of the network had been suspended, elsewhere passengers continued to be shuttled around the great city. Londoners carried on about their business, unaware of the mythic drama unfolding beneath their feet. *Life goes on*, Yaz thought.

'Graham, come in, please,' the Doctor said into her Aénaos phone. 'Comms check. Can you hear me?'

'Roger that, Doctor. Receiving you loud and clear,' came the reply.

Panos clapped his hands in delight. 'The game is afoot! So, Doctor, how do you propose we track down the beast?'

'We're going to draw it out just like King Minos did.' She paused. 'With a human sacrifice.'

9. Minos the Gap

Ryan looked at Yaz's shocked face and gulped. The Doctor's suggestion was as unexpected as it was unwelcome, but it had at least wiped the grin off Panos's chops.

'When I say human sacrifice, I don't mean we're actually going to let it eat anyone. At least, not on purpose. The Minotaur is programmed to behave like a guard, so my guess is that the first thing it's going to do when faced with an intruder is chase them away. And that's how we'll catch it. We're going to dangle some tempting bait in front of its snout.'

'So one of us needs to be the bait?' said Yaz.

'Yup.' The Doctor nodded, rested the sword on the floor and pointed both of her thumbs at her own chest. 'Me, to be exact.'

'No way,' said Yaz.

'It's my plan,' said the Doctor. 'I'm not putting any of you in unnecessary danger.'

Yaz gestured to their surroundings. 'Uh, I think we're way beyond that, don't you? And, anyway, what does this bait have to do – run like the clappers, yeah? Well, I've seen you run. You're old and slow.'

'Cheek!'

'I'm the fastest,' Yaz insisted. 'I should be the bait.'

'She's right,' said Panos, leaning over and picking up the sword. 'Doctor, your role in this is more pivotal than to be the cheese in the trap.'

'I wasn't exactly calling myself a lump of cheddar,' mumbled Yaz, put out.

'More like *gorgon*-zola, eh?' Graham's voice chortled through the phone.

Reluctantly, the Doctor conceded the argument. 'All right. I don't like it but, Yaz, you *are* speedier than a Dalek on a skateboard. I'll give you that.'

'There are two tunnels,' Ryan reminded them. 'And, since we have no idea which one the Minotaur's likely to be hiding down, Yaz can't be the only bait.' He swallowed. 'I'll take the second tunnel.'

'No,' Graham's voice leaped from the phones. 'Out of the question.'

'I can do this,' Ryan said, bristling at the put-down and feeling unusually confident in his physical prowess.

'Ryan, are you sure?' asked the Doctor, her voice conveying an unspoken thought.

Ryan knew what she was getting at. He was dyspraxic, a condition that affected his co-ordination. In the context of being chased by a Minotaur, it made tripping and falling more likely.

He nodded. 'It's all good, Doctor.'

'Take my dogs for added protection,' said Panos. Scylla and Charybdis clung to his heels like shadows, but with a word from him they detached themselves and trotted over to Ryan and Yaz, taking up positions at their sides.

'We have our bait,' said Panos. 'What's the rest of the plan?'

The Doctor held out the spool of steel cable. 'Now we lay Ariadne's golden thread.'

As well as closing the station, Panos had also organised for the track in and round it to be turned off, which meant there was no risk of electrocution from the high voltage running through the outer rails. The Doctor and the others headed down on to the track and together they unspooled the cable, clipping lengths of it across the mouth of the southbound and northbound tunnels at ankle height. They repeated this at regular intervals throughout the tunnels, creating nearly invisible hurdles.

'Ever been to the running of the bulls in Pamplona?' the Doctor asked as they set the cable in place. 'That's what gave me the idea.'

'What happens in Pamplona?' asked Ryan.

'Six bulls are let loose in a fenced-off section of the old city. Then brave – or rash – individuals allow themselves to be chased by the bulls through the streets. It's part of a summer festival.'

'Think I prefer Glastonbury,' muttered Ryan.

'Are the runners ever trampled or gored?' Yaz asked.

'Frequently,' replied the Doctor breezily. 'So, the Minotaur takes the bait, chases you down the tunnel, clipping the cable as it goes, slowing it down and making sure you remain one step ahead. You just have to remember to jump.'

'Wonderful,' said Panos. 'It's like that other ancient Greek tradition, the Olympic hurdles.'

'Don't remember Edwin Moses being chased by a bloomin' great bull,' Graham's unhappy voice moaned.

The Doctor took the opportunity to check in with him high up in the eyrie of the ticket office. 'Spot anything in the tunnels yet?'

'Nope. Not unless you count a rat.'

They clipped the final length of tripwire across the track, and the Doctor addressed Yaz and Ryan once more. 'Once clear of the tunnels, you need to lead the Minotaur back up on to the platform and along the corridor. Then we trap it in a cage, where I will be waiting with the sword, ready to deactivate it.'

'Where are we going to get a cage to hold a Minotaur?' asked Ryan, who hadn't seen anything like that in the equipment they'd assembled for the mission.

'Ever notice what happens to your phone signal when you get in a lift?' said the Doctor.

Sure, the question sounded random, Ryan thought, but he was used to the Doctor's ways by now. She liked to throw in a conversational handbrake turn or two.

'It drops out,' said Yaz.

The Doctor nodded. 'The lift we came down in, like most lifts, exhibits the properties of what's known as a Faraday cage. A container made of a material able to block electromagnetic fields. We know that our Minotaur's engine draws its power from an external source, but once inside the lift and helped by a boost from this –' she twirled her sonic screwdriver – 'it will be cut off from that source. That should weaken it just enough to let me deactivate it with the Sword of Aegeus. As soon as I slot it into place, Bob's your *theios*. That's ancient Greek for uncle.'

Having laid out her strategy for capturing and subduing the Minotaur, the Doctor beamed at the others with an expression that said, 'What could possibly go wrong?'

Yaz gazed steadily at her. 'Remember on Solaria Prime when you tried outwitting that race of hyper-intelligent vampire slugs using a bicycle pump and I said it was the worst plan I'd ever heard?'

'Yes.'

'I was wrong.'

10. Running with the Bull

The Doctor stood outside the open lift, making final preparations for the Minotaur's arrival and capture. Panos watched her unscrew the metal panel that held the call button. Once clear of its mounting, she inspected the coil of wires connecting the button to the door mechanism.

'What do you mean, there's no hatch in the ceiling?' Graham's puzzled voice queried from the Doctor's phone.

The wires sparked as the Doctor held her sonic to them.

'There's always a hatch in the ceiling of a lift,' Graham persisted. 'In every film ever.'

93

'Sorry, Graham,' said the Doctor, concentrating on her task. 'It's one of those movie myths. They haven't fitted them for years because they worked out that the safest place you can be, should a lift experience a mechanical failure, is inside the car.'

'Where you'll be trapped alongside an angry Minotaur,' he added pointedly. 'Yaz is right. This is a terrible plan.'

The Doctor finished her work and turned to Panos. 'I know you want to be Theseus in this scenario but, as much as it may go against your ingrained notions of masculinity, I'm going to ask you to hand over the sword.'

Panos hesitated before offering the weapon to her, hilt-first. 'You're a fascinating woman, Doctor.'

'You have no idea.' She took the blade. 'Once the Minotaur is inside the car with me, it's imperative that it doesn't escape before I have a chance to use the sword. I've rigged the call button so that one press will instantly close the doors.' She demonstrated, giving the button a firm push. The lift doors slammed together like a steel trap. 'That's your job.'

'I usually have someone to push my buttons for me,' said Panos, before breaking out his

94

most charming smile yet. 'It would be my pleasure.'

The tunnel wasn't as dark as Yaz had expected. Every few metres lights were fixed to the wall with their primary function being, she supposed, to aid the work of the maintenance crews who kept the network running. However, the glow did nothing to banish the feeling of intense dread. Waiting was the worst part. She'd been in position for a little more than thirty minutes, approximately ten metres inside the tunnel and still within range of the Wi-Fi signal that kept her in touch with the others. She knew from his updates that Ryan was feeling just as anxious in the northbound tunnel. Her nervousness was tempered by a curious impatience. Somewhere in here was the Minotaur, and that meant a confrontation was imminent. The thought imparted a heady mix of fear and excitement.

'Yaz, check in, please.' It was the Doctor with another of her periodic calls.

'Receiving you,' Yaz replied. 'Still no sign of the target.'

'Okay, Yaz. Ryan, how are you doing?'

There was silence for a few seconds. For a moment, Yaz wondered if something was wrong, and then her friend's voice cut through her anxious thoughts.

'I'm here, Doctor.' Ryan's voice sang out. 'I think I saw Graham's rat.' He didn't sound pleased about the encounter.

'Oh, there are hundreds of them down here,' said the Doctor. 'Thousands, actually.'

Ryan cut in. 'Not making it better.' He sighed. 'This is kinda boring. You sure it's working? I mean, how exactly do I act like bait?'

Yaz couldn't help herself. 'You could shout into the darkness how delicious you are.'

She didn't hear his reply, because at that moment she spotted a movement further along the tunnel. Even with the illumination from the wall lights it was hard to make out exactly what had moved, but it was too small to be the Minotaur and too big for a rat. She'd have to move closer to discover more.

'Possible contact,' she said into the phone. 'Definitely not our bronze friend, but I'm heading into the tunnel to investigate.'

'Negative, Yaz,' said the Doctor. 'Stay put.'

Yaz was growing tired of waiting. 'Come on, Doctor,' she pleaded. 'I'm not doing much good just standing here. And every minute we wait is taking us closer to that thing exploding.'

'All right,' the Doctor conceded. 'But don't go towards the light. It could be a train.'

'And don't go too far into the tunnel,' said Panos. 'Much deeper and you'll be out of communications range.'

Acknowledging the warnings, Yaz set off, the robotic dog padding at her side. Panos had called it Scylla. The first time he'd said the name, she'd misheard it as Cilla, but the mention of its chum, Charybdis, had stirred some ancient memory of a school lesson. Scylla and Charybdis were mythical sea hazards: a six-headed monster and a giant whirlpool. In order to navigate the particular straits these hazards occupied, ships had to risk sailing close to one or the other. 'Caught between Scylla and Charybdis' was the proverb. Another way of putting it was 'between the devil and the deep blue sea'. She glanced down at the slab-bodied, spindly-legged robot thrumming with power, glad it was on her side. It picked its way along the tunnel, long legs tip-tapping against the rails of the deactivated track, until it came to a stop and emitted a low growl.

'What is it?' she said, squinting into the semi-darkness. On the ground beside the dog, something reflected the wall lights. Before Yaz took another step, she checked her phone. Out of range, just as Panos had cautioned. She was on her own. She could either turn back or press on. Who was she kidding? Retreat was not an option.

She drew level with the dog and saw, next to it, slumped against the outside track, a figure in a high-visibility jacket. An Underground worker – had to be. Maybe from one of the maintenance teams. He lay on his back, unmoving. Immediately around him, the ground was a darker shade than the rest, coloured by a spreading bloodstain. She had never seen an injury from a bull's horn before, but she had no doubt that was what she was looking at. The man had been gored just beneath his left armpit. Blood bubbled from a fresh wound – which meant the Minotaur couldn't be far away. At least the man was alive. His wide, frightened eyes took in the sight of the young woman before him.

'It's okay,' said Yaz, her police training kicking in. 'You've been injured, but I'm going to help you.'

She needed to apply pressure to his injury and staunch the flow of blood, but she was short of anything suitable to use and searching the pockets of her jeans provided no solution either. She pulled at her jumper, thinking to use it instead. As she untucked it, Scylla extended one foreleg, a long claw flashed and the dog's leg scythed across the material, neatly severing it and leaving Yaz holding a strip. Shaking off her unease at the speed and ferocity of the dog's action, she pressed the makeshift bandage against the wound.

'What's your name?' she asked the man.

'Willis,' he croaked. 'That thing . . .'

He had to be talking about the Minotaur. 'I know. I'm going to get you out of here.' His pulse was thready and he was in danger of losing consciousness. She daren't leave him there while she fetched the others, but moving him was hardly the easier option. He groaned.

'Stay with me, Willis.' She had to keep him talking. Keep him awake. 'I knew a Willis once. Parents were big fans of *Die Hard*. Don't suppose that's where you got your name?'

'My grandpa . . .'

'Your grandpa was Bruce Willis? Cool.'

Scylla swung round with a hiss and click of its metal legs, angling itself to point deeper into the tunnel. It growled again.

Yaz felt a tingling sensation in her foot. It was touching one of the rails and, for a moment, she wondered if the power had returned to the track, but it was more of a physical vibration. A sound rang out of the rail, over and over, like hammer strikes.

Or footsteps.

She squinted down the long, curving tunnel. A shadow moved on the wall.

The Minotaur was coming, its broad metal feet pounding against the track.

'Up you get, Willis,' Yaz said, helping him to stand. He moaned in pain, but she had no choice. They had to move. Now. Slipping one of his arms round her neck, she supported him as best she could. 'Stay,' she commanded the robotic dog. 'I don't know if you can understand me, but I want you to hold that thing at bay. Got it?' She paused, hoping for some response, but none came. 'Good dog,' she added anyway.

Half dragging the wounded Willis, she hobbled off down the tunnel towards the relative safety of the station. She cursed the tripwires. Intended to slow the Minotaur, now they only served to hinder her progress. Instead of hurdling them as planned, she had to stop at each one and heave Willis over the obstacle. Meanwhile, she could hear the creature drawing inexorably closer. She risked a glance back and immediately wished she hadn't. The thing seemed to fill the tunnel, bronze body flickering like fire as it crashed past the wall lights.

Scylla slid from the shadows to block its path.

The mechanical dog reared up on its hind legs, forming a shape almost as monstrous as the Minotaur's.

Yaz pressed on, making the most of whatever time Scylla might have bought her. At her back, she heard the two combatants clash, bronze against carbon fibre. The sound echoed like ringing swords. Yaz glimpsed the end of the tunnel ahead. She should be back in Wi-Fi range. But, as she reached for her phone, Willis stumbled, causing her to spill the handset. It bounced off the track with a terrible crack and landed face up, its screen shattered.

From behind her came the twang of snapping wire.

The Minotaur had passed Scylla and caught the first tripwire. It barely slowed.

Another snap as it broke through the next.

Willis let out a pained gurgle. 'Can't go on.'

Yaz wasn't having any of that. The mouth of the tunnel was up ahead, close enough now that someone might hear her. She filled her lungs with a great gulp of musty underground air and shouted her head off.

11. Hanging by a Thread

'Graham!' hissed Ryan.

'What?' came the puzzled response from his grandpa.

'You're humming it *again*.'

'Sorry.' He sighed. 'Blame the Doc. Ever since she mentioned it, I can't get it out of my head.'

There was a lengthy pause, during which Ryan hoped that Graham had got the message, but then he started once more, absent-mindedly humming 'Do You Want to Build a Snowman?'

This is totally boring, Ryan thought, as he tried to shut out the terrible sound of Graham's singing. He was in a hurry, burning to get on with something exciting. Though he'd never admit it aloud, he couldn't wait to get in the game and confront that big metal monster. Right now he felt as though he could outrun Usain Bolt.

'HELP! DOCTOR! RYAN!'

It was Yaz, and she was in trouble. Ryan sprinted out of the tunnel, Charybdis keeping pace alongside him. He leaped on to the platform and dashed across to the other side. He was about to jump down on to the track when he saw her. She was hobbling along between the rails, one arm round some bloke with blood pouring down his chest.

A great bellow erupted from the darkness of the tunnel behind her. And it wasn't the southbound to Morden.

'Ryan, help me with him.' Yaz scrambled to the edge of the platform.

Between the two of them, they manoeuvred the injured man on to the platform. He lay there, moaning in pain. Yaz clambered up after him, and Ryan could tell that the physical effort of the rescue had taken it out of her. She could barely put one foot in front of the other. Her eyes flicked to his with the unspoken understanding that they were in deep trouble.

The Minotaur erupted from the mouth of the tunnel.

Ryan couldn't move. In nightmares, monsters always seemed to move with unjust ease, while you, the dreamer, remained stuck; no matter how frenzied your strokes, you couldn't escape the gnashing teeth unless you woke up. But there was no waking up from this.

Thankfully, the mechanical dog didn't appear to have bad dreams. There was a blur of movement as Charybdis launched itself through the air and crashed against the bronze creature's solid chest. The Minotaur raised a massive hand and swiped the dog aside. Robust programming caused Charybdis to pull its legs into its body in a defensive posture, but still it hit the side wall with a denting crunch. With no further obstacle to its progress, the Minotaur made its way on to the platform.

As it did so, Ryan felt a great wave of heat engulf him. That thing was burning hot.

He glanced across at the tired-out Yaz. There was no way she could outrun it, not in her current state. Ryan, by contrast, had fresh legs. Yaz had led the creature here; now it was his turn to pick up the baton in this most deadly relay race. His first challenge was to get the Minotaur's attention away from Yaz and on to him. Shrugging off the fear-induced paralysis and ignoring Graham's increasingly panicked voice from his phone, he began yelling insults at the monster and waving his arms. His efforts had no effect. Perhaps sensing the weakened prey, the creature marched towards his friend. Somehow, Ryan had to draw it away from her, but how?

And then he knew.

Grabbing the Aénaos phone out of his pocket, he swiped the screen with shaking fingers, searching for the right app. Finding it, he stabbed the icon and, with no time to think, chose the first option on the list presented to him on the front page. He cranked the volume to maximum just as the first notes of the classical piece burst from the surprisingly powerful front-firing speakers.

The Minotaur snapped its head round to look for the source of the music. Its massive horns swung away from Yaz and were now levelled at Ryan. The tips gleamed in the light.

'Come on, ya big bronze muppet! Over here!'

Ryan was vaguely aware of Graham's objections. 'What are you doing? Are you taunting the Minotaur?'

At the same time, his eye fell on the phone screen, glimpsing the name of the composer and the title of the piece. Handel. Sarabande in D Minotaur . . . No, D *Minor.*

The beast lowered its head and charged. Ryan felt a slug of adrenaline hit him, filling him up like rocket fuel.

He flew across the platform, reaching the stairs in seconds, taking them three at a time. The blood roared in his ears, and the Minotaur roared behind him. On down the corridor to the lift, where the Doctor waited. There she was in the doorway. Just outside stood Panos, ready to spring the trap as soon as Ryan led the creature inside. But, as fast as Ryan was, the Minotaur was faster. It was catching him. He knew it was a machine, and yet he was sure he could feel its hot, sour breath on the back of his neck. Last few metres. Sensing the approaching swing of its mighty arm like a shadow on the water, he slipped through the lift doors and flung himself to one side. The Minotaur missed, but its momentum took it inside. It struck the far wall and bounced off. Perhaps sensing the trap, it let out another bellow.

The doors snapped shut.

'Graham, now!' yelled the Doctor. 'Bring us up. The Faraday-cage effect only works when we're not touching the ground.'

The lift jolted into motion, hauling them slowly to the surface. The heat radiating from the Minotaur was already turning the inside of the car into a furnace. Ryan wiped a sleeve across his heavily perspiring brow. He was melting, but somehow the Doctor remained cool, even this close to the fiery monster.

She held the Sword of Aegeus in both hands and calmly lined up her shot. But, as she raised the blade to strike, the Minotaur swung round, its arm knocking the sword from her grip. It went clattering to the floor.

The Minotaur raged, the tips of its wide horns scraping the walls of the lift as it turned its blazing eyes on Ryan. There was nowhere to run. A bronze hand shot towards him like a spear and clasped his neck, fingers tightening round his windpipe. Ryan could feel and hear his skin blister beneath the grill-hot fingers. All at once, the beast picked him up and flung him against one wall. He slammed into the control panel and must have nudged the emergency call button, because a few seconds later a voice came out of the speaker.

'Hello, this is the Lift Maintenance Help Desk. First thing to say is you are perfectly safe.'

With another roar, the Minotaur ripped the control panel off the wall in a tangle of sparking wires.

Blinking sweat from his eyes, Ryan noticed a warning sign on the wall that referred to the lift's maximum load. He guessed they were wildly beyond the recommended limit. The lift cable shrieked its displeasure, and the floor of the car bowed like a trampoline.

'Doc–' Ryan gasped.

Just as he was sure he was about to become a human shish kebab, the Doctor made her move. She had retrieved the sword. Through his fading vision, Ryan glimpsed the puzzling markings along its ancient blade. They blurred as the Doctor plunged the sword into the beast's back.

Instantly the Minotaur froze. A statue once more.

Ryan remained in its grip, but was able to gather enough breath to prevent himself from blacking out. He felt a surge of relief. 'Doctor, you did it!' he gasped. 'Can you get me out of here now, please?'

She raised her sonic, but before she could fire it there came a crack from the lift cable and the car dropped several metres, before stabilising. It continued to crawl upwards, creaking and popping like a submarine under pressure. The journey down to the platform had taken half a minute, but the climb to the surface promised to be a longer haul.

Ryan swallowed tightly, suddenly aware of a new sensation. 'The hand. It's getting hotter.'

'Ah,' said the Doctor.

He did not like the sound of that.

'Remember when I said the phrase on the sword was "come to an end"? I was right, but my Nimon might have been a bit rusty. It is "come to an end", but not as in "deactivate". More like . . . "destruct".'

'Doc, are we winning?' Graham's voice asked hopefully from Ryan's Aénaos phone.

The Doctor sniffed. 'The Minotaur has Ryan in a death grip, but don't worry. It'll almost certainly explode before it gets a chance to throttle him.'

Graham let out a whimper.

'How long?' Yaz this time. Despite its screen being shattered, her phone was still functioning.

Ryan was glad to have her close, even if it was just her voice.

The Doctor passed her sonic screwdriver across the motionless body of the Minotaur. 'Call it an even sixty seconds.'

'I'm setting a timer,' said Yaz. 'Sixty and counting . . .'

In the tiny lift, there was no room for the Doctor to pace, so instead she tapped her foot against the buckled floor, running through her options. 'I could try reprogramming the sword with the correct instructions. But I only have basic tourist Nimon. I can just about order a cappuccino. So that's a non-starter.'

Ryan could feel the fiery bronze burning his neck.

The Doctor rapped a knuckled fist against her skull. 'Think. Think! It has one port on the back for the programmable sword and draws its power remotely. That's what brought us to Earth in the first place. But, if I was in the business of constructing a killer robotic temple guard, I'd include a back-up method of charging. Something direct. A plug socket.' Urgently, she pressed her hands to the bronze skin and ran them across its body. 'And, if I was being all Greek and poetic, I'd put it right . . . here.' Her fingers found a faint seam on the middle-left of its chest. 'The heart.'

A quick press released a spring-loaded catch, opening a rectangular section of the chest cavity about the size of a human hand. Beneath the outer cover, six screws held a second cover in place. The Doctor immediately applied her sonic. 'So rare these days that I get to use it as an *actual* screwdriver.'

One by one, the screws popped out, falling to the floor and ringing off the metal surface.

'Thirty seconds,' Yaz announced.

The last screw fell away, rolling across the floor and coming to rest against the doors. Beyond the discomfort caused by the stranglehold, Ryan noted that the lift was at an odd angle and was continuing to make terrible noises as the cable strained to haul them to the surface.

The Doctor prised open the inner cover of the chest cavity and was faced with the dark heart of the Minotaur. From his position, Ryan got a good look at the mechanism. It was similar to the one he'd found on the TARDIS – a collection of tiny cogs set within an ancient stone, but with a filigreed tangle of arteries and veins in gold and silver branching off, presumably to carry vital power around the body.

'Twenty seconds . . .'

'Just have to remove it. Very carefully.' The Doctor peered into the cavity, cautiously inserted her hand and closed it round the stone heart. She began to ease it out, but stopped almost immediately. 'Wait. It's too easy.'

Struggling for breath, Ryan nonetheless managed to blurt out, 'Are you kidding me?'

'The Minoans were known for their love of booby-traps. If I break any of these gold or silver connectors, I suspect the whole thing is designed to go off immediately. There must be a release mecha–'

Before she could finish, there was a terrible snap and Ryan felt his body go weightless. In that instant he knew what had happened: overwhelmed by the weight in the car, the lift cable had finally given way, and they were plunging down the shaft. Every detail around him suddenly became vivid and sharp. There could only be seconds before impact, and yet time seemed to stretch out. He felt pressure building in his ears as the air screamed around the plummeting lift. The Doctor seemed remarkably calm, as if defusing an ancient bomb while hurtling nearly sixty metres down a lift shaft was nothing out of the ordinary.

'Ten seconds, Doctor!' Yaz's voice sounded far away.

The Doctor squinted into the cavity. A single golden vein snaked up the wide throat and into the head.

Ryan couldn't imagine things getting any worse, but he was wrong. He watched in horror as the heart started ticking once more. A cogwheel rotated, setting in motion the rest of the mechanism. The Minotaur was slowly stirring, and he felt the first twitch of its fingers. Maybe the Doctor was wrong, and it *would* have time to throttle him before exploding.

'Five seconds . . .'

The Doctor turned her attention to the creature's unblinking eye.

'Four . . .'

There was something round the socket. A bezel – the sort of thing you'd find on the circumference of a diver's watch.

'Three . . .'

She gripped it between her fingers and turned.

'Two . . .'

The heart popped out of its cavity and landed in her outstretched palm. The awakening Minotaur sank back, finally releasing Ryan from its grip. The heart gave one last tick and fell silent, just as the lift's safety measures kicked in. Ryan felt the strong hand of decelerating forces as the car came to a controlled stop.

'One,' he squeaked, before dropping to the buckled floor and kissing it gratefully.

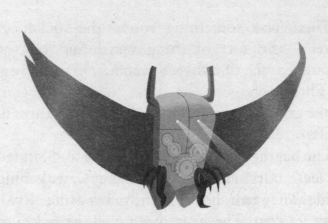

12. Take the Boy

Graham waited impatiently at the surface level. He'd lost the camera feed inside the car when it started to fall, but a brief, relieved call with Yaz had filled him in on the events of the past few minutes. They were on their way up from the platform in the one remaining working lift. Everyone was safe, although the maintenance man Yaz had found in the tunnel needed medical assistance. Graham had asked the police officers at the station entrance to call for an ambulance. One was on its way. He glanced towards the street entrance to see if it had arrived yet.

There was no ambulance, but he watched uneasily as a different vehicle glided to a stop. Its high-sided proportions resembled an ambulance, but instead of a London Ambulance Service logo it sported the same Aénaos symbol that was on all the phones. The back doors flew open, disgorging half a dozen figures wearing full-body hazmat suits. Sunlight reflected off clear visors, obscuring the faces of the people inside the suits. At least, Graham assumed there were people inside. They marched into the ticket office.

'Evacuate the area,' commanded the figure in the lead, who carried a lockbox with a prominent radiation symbol. 'We are investigating a potential radiobiological hazard.'

Unnerved at the mention of such a thing, the police officers complied, promptly pulling back to a position on the street outside the station. Graham couldn't blame them, but he wasn't so easily dislodged. Another figure entered the ticket hall. It was Penelope Polichroniadis.

On her shoulder, wings folded into its body, sat a large owl. Graham blinked. Definitely an owl, though on closer inspection he saw that it wasn't alive. It reminded him of the mechanical dogs – the same perfectly smooth composite-material construction, but this time formed into a sleek body, ear-shaped antennae and powerful black talons. Where its eyes should have been was instead a pair of red laser-scanners.

'What's going on?' Graham asked Penelope.

At first she didn't even register his presence, his protests being of no more interest to her than the objections of a mouse would have been to the predator on her shoulder.

'Don't pretend you've forgotten who I am,' he said. 'My grandson looked after you when you were injured.'

The mention of Ryan got her attention. As she turned her head to Graham, so did the owl. It was as if they were connected by an invisible wire.

'This is not your concern,' she said coolly.

Graham was outraged. 'My friends just stopped a walking nuclear bomb from going off in the Tube –'

'And we will deal with it from here.'

Just then the lift arrived and, with a jangle of the alarm, the doors parted. Inside were the Doctor, Ryan, Yaz and Panos. Between them they carried a man, who Graham assumed to be the injured maintenance worker.

Several of the waiting hazmat-suited figures produced small firearms and, at gunpoint, beckoned the Doctor and her companions into the ticket hall.

'Here, what's going on?' demanded Graham.

'I think it's called a double-cross,' said the Doctor. She clutched what Graham figured must be the Minotaur's heart.

Panos extended a hand. 'I believe that belongs to me.'

'I outbid you for it,' the Doctor reminded him.

An expression of puzzlement clouded Panos's features. A man unused to being outspent, he had assumed that the item, like everything else in his life, belonged to him.

'You will be recompensed,' he offered.

'I don't want your money,' the Doctor said – but, staring into the muzzle of a semi-automatic pistol, she had no option. Grudgingly, she placed the heart into his palm. 'I wouldn't recommend using it as a desk ornament. It's still highly unstable.'

Panos took the heart and carefully laid it into a perfectly shaped compartment in the open lockbox. He closed the lid and there was a series of clicks and hisses as it was sealed up inside. 'This will keep it safe.'

The Doctor studied the box for a moment. 'Purpose-built to fit the heart, with walls that restrict the mechanism's ability to draw external power. You don't just grab something like that off the shelf – you had to have it ready. Which means this isn't the first one of these devices you've come across.'

Panos grinned. 'Very clever, Doctor.'

'It's time to leave,' snapped Penelope, interrupting her star-struck brother. She nodded at two members of her team. 'Take the boy.'

Immediately they grabbed Ryan's arms.

'Hey! What're you doing? Get off me.'

Graham bristled with fury. 'No way. You're taking my grandson over my dead body.'

'I wouldn't make idle threats,' Penelope said coldly.

Ignoring her, Graham took an angry step towards Ryan's captors.

At the same time, the robot owl took off from Penelope's shoulder and flew towards him. A single flap of its black wings launched it across the ticket hall. Black talons outstretched, it swooped down and ran them across Graham's cheek, drawing blood. With a cry of pain, he stopped in his tracks. The bird circled once and returned to its perch.

It was a warning shot, but the deadly implication of the attack was clear. 'Put the boy in the car,' ordered Penelope.

'There are two police officers outside this

118

station, and one inside,' said Yaz, referring to herself. 'We're not going to let you kidnap Ryan in broad daylight.'

A dismissive expression crossed Penelope's face. 'Don't you understand yet? In this world no one has the power to deny us *anything*.'

'See, there's your problem,' said the Doctor. 'I'm not from this world. And I've been threatened by a lot worse than you. You should know that there isn't anywhere in space or time you can hide that I won't find you. Ryan, we're coming for you. Hold tight.'

'You misunderstand, Doctor,' said Panos. 'This is for the boy's own good. We want to cure him –'

'Enough!' Penelope shut down her brother. She snapped her fingers, and the hazmat team headed for the exit, taking Ryan with them.

'What're you on about?' Ryan objected as he was led away. 'There's nothing wrong with me.'

Panos gave a long whistle. There was a clicking sound from the entrance to the emergency staircase that spiralled down to the platform level, then Scylla and Charybdis hobbled into the ticket hall. Both robot bodies were dented and one of them had lost a leg. Ignoring the Doctor and the others, they trailed after their owners.

Panos gazed at the Doctor. 'I do wish we could part on more amicable terms, but I regret that circumstances force me down this path.' His words expressed regret, but his tone bordered on gleeful. With a formal bow, he turned to follow his sister.

'It's okay, Graham,' Ryan called over his shoulder. 'Don't worry about me.'

His attempt at reassurance failed to have the desired effect on his grandpa or the others.

'Can't you do something?' Yaz whispered urgently to the Doctor.

She watched them leave. 'All in good time.'

There was no point in reporting Ryan's abduction to the police, since the Polichroniadis siblings exerted too much influence over the authorities. And a quick visit to the mansion house established what the Doctor had already guessed: Panos and Penelope were no longer home. Graham couldn't hide his anxiety. Where were they, and what did they have in store for Ryan?

'What did he mean by "curing" him?' Graham hadn't got over Panos's odd pronouncement. That and the presence of the men in hazmat suits had instilled in him a feeling of dread. 'Ryan's not sick, is he?'

'He'll be fine,' said Yaz. 'He *is* fine. In fact, I can't remember him being better. The way he shot off with that Minotaur on his tail – didn't think he had it in him. Right, Doctor?'

The Doctor remained silent. It was clear to Graham that she was mentally working through their options, though he wished that she could have offered him some comfort.

After ensuring that the injured Tube worker had been taken care of, they returned to the TARDIS to plan their next move. The Doctor searched the ship's database for information about Panos and Penelope that might lead to their current whereabouts. Yaz and Graham hovered at her shoulder as she entered the search parameters.

'The TARDIS database does whereabouts *and* whenabouts,' the Doctor explained. 'We should be able to pinpoint them in space and time.'

A screed of biographical information scrolled past, charting the rise of the Polichroniadis pair.

'So this is how they made all that money,' the Doctor remarked. 'Aénaos phones.'

The Aénaos brand belonged to the siblings. The phones had appeared just under a decade ago, blazing on to the market with a remarkable selling point: the batteries never ran out of charge.

'Aénaos. Perpetual. Quite a boast,' said the Doctor.

'But that's impossible,' said Yaz when she'd finished reading the section on screen. 'Isn't it?'

The Doctor was staring into space, deep in thought. 'Why did Panos want the Minotaur's heart? Because he recognised it, that's why. He knew precisely what he was chasing.' She snapped out of her daydream and produced the handset that Panos had given her. She studied it from all angles, then she dropped it to the floor. Lifting one booted foot, she stomped down on it, cracking the case and spilling its insides. Kneeling among the scattered components, she fished out one small section about the size of a thumbnail.

Yaz peered at it in surprise. 'It looks like the Minotaur's heart. Only smaller.'

The Doctor nodded. 'Produced using modern manufacturing processes, but definitely reverse-engineered.'

Graham tried to get his head round what she was saying. 'So, the only way to make one of these would be if you already possessed an original?'

'They lied to us,' said Yaz.

'Looks like phones were just the start,' said the Doctor, indicating a fresh piece of information on screen. 'According to this, Panos and Penelope have been working on another project. A power plant. They're calling it the first of a revolutionary breed of generator that will provide clean energy for the planet. This is a news report from the official switch-on, which happens two days in the future.' The Doctor began programming the navigation system. 'That's where and when we'll find them.'

13. The Talos Project

As the helicopter shot out of the valley and banked hard to skirt yet another mountainous peak, Ryan felt his stomach lurch. He was still suffering from the after-effects of whatever drug it was they'd dosed him with shortly after his abduction. In the car as they drove him from the Tube, he remembered the glint of a hypodermic needle, then nothing until he awoke aboard a private jet. It had taken a few moments for his vision to settle. At first glance, he'd thought he was alone in the luxurious quiet of the passenger compartment, but then he saw one of those creepy mechanical dogs sitting on its haunches in the aisle.

A glance out of the window had revealed a cloud-capped mountain range below, but not for long. The drug was still in his system and it took hold of him again, dragging him back down into unconsciousness. He didn't know how long he'd been out since then, but he was pretty sure they were the same high and snowy mountains that he was now passing through in a helicopter.

At the controls, Panos let out a whoop of delight at his reckless aerobatic manoeuvring. Beside him, Penelope sat impassively.

As yet, Ryan had no idea what they wanted with him, or where they were taking him. *We wish only to cure you.* That's what Penelope had said back in London, just before he glimpsed the needle. But he felt fine. Maybe a bit hotter than usual, but hardly anything to be concerned about. This was a whole lot of trouble to go to for a temperature.

Ryan closed his eyes and tried to focus on something else – anything to take his mind off the roller-coaster flight through the mountains. Unfortunately, the only thing that came to mind was that, since meeting the Doctor, he had been abducted on four separate occasions. Until meeting her, zero times. Since . . . four. This would make five. Assuming he survived this encounter, the logical thing would be to quit.

Say goodbye, walk out of the TARDIS door and never look back. It was insane the amount of danger he'd been exposed to in the short time he'd travelled with the Doctor: giant spiders, flesh-eating moths, a Dalek. And that was barely scratching the sonic-mined surface.

The helicopter pitched at an alarming angle, climbing rapidly and leaving Ryan's stomach somewhere far below. He swallowed hard to clear the sudden pressure in his ears. Despite everything, he wouldn't have missed his adventures for the world – not for any of the numerous and dangerous worlds he'd visited. Neil Armstrong might have taken one small step on to the Moon but, thanks to the Doctor, Ryan Sinclair's trainers had taken giant leaps all over the universe.

He clung to the one constant he could be sure of, which was that even now the TARDIS would be winging its way to his rescue. In fact, given that it was a time machine, the Doctor and the others were probably already waiting for him, no doubt with a brilliant plan to outwit Panos and Penelope.

Panos steadied the craft, levelling it off and handing the controls to his sister. As he turned his head, Ryan noticed the grey pallor of his face. Sweat beaded on his forehead.

'What's wrong with him?' asked Ryan.

'He is cursed,' said Penelope, eyes fixed straight ahead. 'Like you.'

Unnerved, Ryan didn't have time to ask more before he felt the helicopter change course again. It was descending, smoothly this time. Beneath them, on a mountain plateau, he could make out a landing pad.

An emergency medical team was waiting when they touched down. Physicians in Aénaos uniforms whisked off the stricken Panos. Meanwhile, ground crew tended to the helicopter and unloaded the cargo. They had travelled light from London, the only notable luggage – apart from Ryan – the box containing the mechanism the Doctor had ejected from the Minotaur.

'This way,' ordered Penelope, setting off downhill. Ryan turned to follow her and stopped almost immediately. There, beyond the landing pad, seemingly carved into the side of the mountain, lay what appeared to be the entrance to an ancient stone temple.

'Do you know the ancient Greek myth of Talos?' asked Penelope.

It was some time later that day Ryan couldn't be sure how long had passed, since time was difficult to keep track of in here. It was something to do with the lack of windows. After Penelope

127

had expertly steered the helicopter to safety, she had gone off with her ailing brother while Ryan was taken through the temple entrance and delivered here. It was some kind of medical clinic located inside the mountain. In contrast to the exterior, it was bright and modern, the most ancient thing about it the magazines in the waiting room. A nurse had drawn some blood, noted down various things including his temperature and blood pressure, shone a light in his eyes and then deposited him back in the waiting room. He'd been reading a copy of *BBC Top Gear* when Penelope reappeared. She commanded him to follow her, leading him further into the bustling clinic.

The name Talos meant nothing to him, so he shook his head and let her continue. That weird stuff in the helicopter about a curse had left him uneasy, and he was desperate to know the truth about what was going on. If he had to sit through an ancient history lesson first, that was okay. And, if he was being honest, he kind of liked Penelope.

She began her story. 'The legend says that Talos was a creature of bronze made by Hephaestus, the god of fire and iron. It was presented to King Minos as a gift to protect the island of Crete from invaders. Talos would stand like a tower on the cliffs overlooking the sea. When he spied enemy ships, he would hurl great rocks at them, splintering their wooden hulls and sending them to the bottom of the Aegean. But sometimes they would evade his missiles and make it to land, which was unfortunate . . . for them. Because Talos had an even more terrible power. He would make his metal body as hot as a furnace and clasp the invaders in his arms, burning them to death.'

They reached a large round door and Penelope placed her hand on a pad set into the wall next to it. Some kind of biometric reader, Ryan guessed, as at her touch the door unlocked and slowly hinged open. They went through.

'But Talos was no myth. He was an ordinary man who encountered an alien artefact. An artefact identical to the one you and the Doctor retrieved from the Minotaur statue.'

'The stone engine?' said Ryan.

'It exploded and a fragment lodged itself in his body. The fragment continued to function like the engine it had once been a part of, generating energy, but now doing it *inside* his body. The effect of which was to make him restless and cause his temperature to soar uncontrollably. The only way to moderate the heat was to encase him in a purpose-built suit of bronze. Some speculate that the design for the suit came from the brilliant mind of an inventor called Daedalus, but how and why is lost to us now. It seems the suit was able to regulate the occupant's temperature, keeping him alive. But, eventually, he had a choice to make: a life encased in bronze, or a limited time free from its constraints. He chose the latter and took off the suit for the last time.' Penelope fell quiet for a moment. 'Even the great Daedalus was unable to find a permanent cure. But that's what we are trying to do here.'

They struck off along a passage lined with numbered doors.

As fascinating as the Talos story was, and as happy as he was to spend time in Penelope's company, Ryan had one question. 'What does any of this have to do with me?'

'The first time we met I looked into your eyes,' said Penelope.

Knew it! He remembered the moment with total clarity. He hadn't imagined it – that lingering look meant she fancied him.

'I saw it,' she continued. 'You have a piece of the stone engine in your left eye.'

Oh. His disappointment at not being the object of her affection was quickly replaced by confusion and fear. When the stone engine aboard the TARDIS had exploded, he'd initially wondered if a splinter had embedded itself but, since he hadn't felt any irritation, he'd dismissed the notion.

'The symptoms are a high temperature coupled with hyperactivity. You feel as if you're burning with energy. Which, in fact, you are.'

That was how he had been feeling since that moment in the TARDIS. Could it be true?

'The tests we performed when you arrived confirm it. I'm sorry.' Penelope laid a hand on Ryan's and squeezed. 'But that's why we brought you here – to cure you.'

She stopped outside one of the doors. As she reached for the handle, the strange words she'd spoken aboard the helicopter came back to Ryan. *He is cursed, like you.*

'The same thing happened to Panos, didn't it? That's why he collapsed in the helicopter?'

She nodded. 'Panos was once a watchmaker on Crete. One day, a fisherman brought him something he'd caught in one of his nets. To the fisherman it appeared to be some kind of clock mechanism, but Panos recognised in it something far more powerful. It was a stone engine, washed up from the seabed where it had lain for four thousand years. Panos paid the fisherman for it and began to study its workings. The engine granted us riches beyond our imagination. But the ancient technology that made our fortune also cursed my brother. It exploded and sent a shard into his eye.'

Penelope went inside the room and Ryan followed her. It was an otherwise ordinary hospital room, but in the centre lay a golden sarcophagus just like the one Ryan had seen Panos appear from back in the London house. Penelope pushed a control in the wall and the lid began to rise.

'Like Talos,' she went on, 'my brother began to experience the same symptoms. But, thanks to our new-found wealth, we were able to build him what we call a Daedalus box.' She gestured to the sarcophagus. 'But, as you have heard, that is no long-term solution. We have spent half our fortune searching for a cure. We collect objects like the Minotaur, which contain examples of the technology, hoping to find a clue.'

'What about an operation to remove the fragment?' said Ryan.

'It appears that, once embedded in a human body, the fragment fuses itself with the subject, effectively turning the body into an engine. Unfortunately, no human body can survive that amount of energy flowing through it. Not for long. Over the years, we have attempted different surgical techniques, new treatments, but the outcome remains the same in every case. Fatal.'

Ryan swallowed. That did not sound good. At all.

'Please do not worry. We have a new solution that promises great success.'

Reassured for the moment, Ryan expressed his surprise at how many people had fallen prey to the exploding stone engines. 'It's not like they're lying about all over the place.'

Penelope hesitated before speaking again. 'No. The engines are rare, and the problem more so. That's why we have had to re-create my brother's condition in others.'

It took a second for Ryan to comprehend what she was saying. 'You do this to people? Blow those things up in their faces?'

'Nothing so random. We implant the subjects with pieces of the mechanism. The insertion is simple enough. Regrettably, none have survived the extraction process.'

Ryan was disgusted.

'I see you disapprove.' Penelope rounded on him, those violet eyes of hers flashing. 'But tell me this: how far would you go to save the life of someone you love?' She stroked his cheek and he recoiled at her now-unwelcome touch. 'That's what makes you so special. Like my brother, not only did your condition come about accidentally, but the fragment in each of you is in precisely the same place.' She smiled. 'That makes you the perfect test subject. *You* are our solution. If the new procedure works on you, then it will work on Panos.'

Ryan held up his hands and started to back out of the room. 'Whoa! You're not testing anything on me.'

'But, without treatment, you will heat up until your heart explodes in your chest.'

'Know what? I'll take my chances.'

He turned to flee, but found his way blocked by a couple of burly orderlies wearing Aénaos uniforms. Before he knew what was happening, they had pinned his arms to his sides and were guiding him back into the room.

'Hey! Get off me!'

He struggled in vain as they hauled him towards the open casket. With surprisingly little effort, they picked him up, his legs still kicking, and laid him down inside. The shock of the ice-cold metal against his back took his breath away.

'Penelope, don't do this.' His teeth chattered. 'Please.'

It was already too late. The lid began to close, engulfing him in shadow. Very soon, only a crack of light remained and then, with a thud, it too had gone, and Ryan was left in darkness.

14. Climb Ev'ry Mountain

Their destination was in Switzerland, near the Austrian border, two days along their current timeline. The Doctor had said that the power plant was in the Alps but, until the TARDIS was on its final approach, Yaz hadn't realised she meant it was *inside* an alp.

A moment ago, the granite peak had been a snowy dot on the horizon. Now, as they hurtled towards it at mind- and space-bending speeds, it filled the screen on the timeship's internal display.

Graham eyed the fast-approaching mountain warily. 'Uh, shouldn't we be magically materialising inside the mountain about now?'

'Magic? Magic's got nothing to do with it,' snipped the Doctor as she worked the controls. 'The TARDIS is one of the universe's greatest scientific triumphs, a perfect symphony of mind and technology, the pinnacle of the Time Lords' – uh-oh.'

The TARDIS juddered and the rising and falling time-rotor in the centre of the console froze.

'Something inside the mountain is interfering with the navigation system. We're going down.'

Graham clasped his hands together and placed them on top of his head. 'Brace! Brace!'

'We're not crashing, Graham.'

'Word of advice, Doc. Better choice of phrase next time.'

'Yeah. We're just landing –' she lowered her voice – 'hard.'

With a collective yell, they veered off course, sliding so close to the craggy rock face that Yaz was sure she snatched sight of a very surprised mountain goat.

'Ready?' said the Doctor, hands poised over the controls like a concert pianist about to play the final notes of a symphony. 'Here it comes. One, two, three and . . .'

Graham winced, preparing for an impact that never came.

'Hey presto!' the Doctor declared.

Graham threw her a dark look.

They had materialised in a valley at the foot of the mountain range. The TARDIS had touched down on the edge of a well-paved road above a small village. Neat wooden houses with peaked roofs clustered around a church at the centre. On one side of the village, alpine meadows shone with colourful wildflowers; on the other glowered a dense green pine forest. A freshening breeze swirled through the valley, ruffling the stalks of grass and rattling the leaves on the trees. The whole place looked to Yaz like something out of a fairy tale. One of the dark ones.

Above them, low cloud straggled across the mountainside, obscuring the distant summit. The road climbed in a series of switchbacks and vertical drops until it disappeared from view. A tricky prospect to drive, but that was irrelevant unless the TARDIS could sprout wheels. As she looked up, Yaz noticed a cable car emerge from the cloud, then travel down towards a point not far away. As it descended past them, she saw the Aénaos logo on the side of the gondola. That was their way into the plant.

It didn't take long to locate the cable-car station. Employees of the company presented identification badges at a security checkpoint and boarded the next car going up. The Doctor flashed her psychic paper to the guard, explaining that she and the others were engineers working at the nearby Large Hadron Collider, here for today's official switch-on. The guard readily accepted the Doctor's bluff, but required names for their security badges.

'This is Doctor Maria von Trapp,' said Graham, indicating the Doctor, before turning to Yaz. 'And this is Yasmin von Trapp, and I am . . .' He paused. 'Captain Graham von Trapp.'

Yaz rolled her eyes, while the security guard appeared slightly puzzled.

'You're a *family* of engineers?' he said.

Yaz dug an elbow into Graham's ribs and hissed in his ear, 'If you say *singing* engineers, I'll arrest you myself.'

The ruse worked and they joined the Aénaos employees in the gondola. The door was closed and locked, a bell rang and the car swiftly began to climb, rising through wispy cloud, leaving the summer meadow far behind. Soon they were arriving at the power station's main entrance. Yaz had expected a modern building, but instead she was faced with an entrance more suited to an ancient temple. Broad pillars of mottled grey stone flanked a soaring doorway, above which was carved the image of a three-headed dog. Beneath it was an inscription in what she assumed to be Greek.

'Does it say, "Abandon all hope, ye who enter"?' Graham asked nervously.

'No,' said the Doctor, 'It reads, "Human ingenuity joined to the force of falling water creates light and power". This place must once have been a hydroelectric power plant.'

'You really think Ryan's in here?' asked Yaz.

The Doctor nodded. 'For some reason he's important to Panos and Penelope. Wherever they are, Ryan won't be far away.'

A woman was waiting for them. She wore Aénaos-branded overalls and a yellow hard hat from which peeked two strands of braided blonde hair. She introduced herself as Heidi, their guide – she would take them to join the other guests and dignitaries for the switch-on.

'You're late,' she said in a brusque Austrian accent.

'Sorry about that,' said the Doctor. 'We had car trouble.'

Heidi explained that the ceremony was due to take place shortly in the main generator hall, but they had to hurry as the venue was located almost three kilometres inside the mountain.

She checked their name badges. 'You must wear these at all times,' she instructed them, adding that the badges were embedded with radio-frequency ID chips, which permitted the wearers limited security clearance within the power plant for the duration of their visit and would also act as personal locators in the event of an emergency.

Briefing over, Heidi led them inside. A rank of open-topped buggies awaited in a spacious vestibule. They climbed aboard the leading one, and Heidi touched her name badge to a panel where the dashboard in a regular car would have been. There was a chime as digital displays pulsed green at her touch, unlocking drive systems. From deep within the chassis came the now-familiar *tick-tick* of a stone engine. Yaz realised that, like the workings of the Aénaos phone, the ancient Minoan technology had been repurposed to power the electric vehicle.

'Main generator hall,' she instructed in a clear voice.

The buggy jolted into motion, near-silent motors quickly gathering speed. As they raced off, Yaz realised that Heidi wasn't driving. The vehicle was steering itself – which meant that they didn't need Heidi in order to reach their destination. Yaz had a sneaking suspicion that the guide was there not so much to assist them as keep an eye on them.

It appeared that the Doctor hadn't noticed, or didn't care. She had something else on her mind, and Yaz had a fair idea what that was. *Car trouble.* Something had knocked the TARDIS off course, and it took a great deal more than a flat tyre to do that. Yaz had no doubt that this mountain was hiding something staggeringly powerful.

The electric buggy whizzed them silently along wide tunnels lit with cool blue LED tubes, which were fixed along the walls.

'You're not burning fossil fuels, and I don't see any sign of nuclear or hydroelectric,' said the Doctor, 'so how are you generating your power?'

'I'm afraid that's proprietary information,' Heidi replied.

'You mean it's your secret sauce?' asked Graham, for clarification.

Heidi smiled at him with the sort of expression reserved for elderly relatives. The blue tunnel gave way to one lit by yellow lights.

The tunnels were vast and deep, the whole place like the burrow of some giant earthworm, thought Yaz. She swiftly quashed the thought, knowing from bitter experience that, in the Doctor's universe, such monsters were perfectly possible.

'You could drive a bus through here,' Graham said with a long, low whistle.

As they shot along the twisting passages, Heidi recounted the history of the power station.

The Doctor had been correct: this place was once the site of a hydroelectric plant, dating to the early twentieth century. The original excavation of the mountain formed the basis of the current layout.

'If we'd built it from scratch,' Heidi explained, 'it wouldn't have the same eccentric layout. This place is like –'

'A maze?' suggested the Doctor.

Heidi looked at her with a curious expression. 'Yes. Precisely.'

'Lot of them about,' said the Doctor, casting a glance at Yaz and Graham. 'So, the colour-coded tunnels are to aid navigation, yeah?'

Yaz realised that the lights were strung along the walls rather like Ariadne's thread.

The Doctor continued. 'Blue for north–south running passages, yellow for east–west?'

Heidi was impressed at the Doctor's grasp of the set-up. 'And the different sectors of the plant have their own colours too. Green for the main generator. Orange for maintenance subsystems –'

'And purple for the medical wing?' said the Doctor.

'Actually, it's red for the clinic,' Heidi corrected her. 'Being so far from the nearest hospital, we operate a medical facility capable of dealing with even the most serious emergency.'

Yaz observed the faintest of smiles flit across the Doctor's lips. Heidi had fallen into her conversational trap, offering up the information she required.

Soon, the buggy slowed to a stop in a green-lit tunnel, pulling up at the back of a rank of empty vehicles parked outside a sleek white door. While Heidi went towards the door, the Doctor took the brief opportunity of her absence to address the others.

'In London, Panos said he wanted to cure Ryan, whatever that means. Well, if you're going to cure someone, you'd take them –'

'To the hospital,' finished Graham, understanding dawning.

The Doctor nodded. 'We can't all go. It'd be too obvious. And, anyway, I have a feeling I need to know what's happening through there.' She gestured to the door.

'I'll find Ryan,' said Graham.

'Follow the red tunnels. And this will help.' The Doctor touched her sonic to his name badge and fired a blast. 'I've increased your security-level clearance. Nothing should get in your way now. *And* you can get free coffee from any vending machine.'

'Doctor, this way, please.' Heidi beckoned from the now-open door, through which, above the background thrum of industrial machinery, came the unexpected blare of trumpets.

The Doctor put an arm round Heidi's shoulder and propelled her inside the generator hall. Yaz watched in admiration as the Doctor kept up a constant chatter, keeping Heidi's focus off Graham, who was already slipping away along the passage in the near-silent electric buggy.

Yaz followed the Doctor into the main hall, towards the arch of an airport-style scanner. Ahead of them, another guest deposited her rings and mobile phone into a tray, which one of two security guards on duty put aside, informing her that she could collect her possessions at the end of the ceremony.

'Apologies for this,' said Heidi to the Doctor and Yaz. 'But the equipment in here is highly sensitive, and we wouldn't want any accidents.'

'Of course not,' said the Doctor, swanning through the arch.

The moment she stepped past the threshold of the machine, there was a high-pitched beep and a red light flashed. One of the guards blocked her path, politely asking her to turn out her pockets.

She pulled out the offending object: her sonic screwdriver.

'My inhaler?' she said hopefully.

Unswayed, the guard extended a tray, into which the Doctor reluctantly dropped the device.

'Never mind,' the Doctor whispered to Yaz. 'I spent an entire regeneration without a sonic screwdriver. Didn't do me any harm.' She paused. 'Mind you, I did waste an awful lot of time trying to break in to and out of locked rooms.'

They followed Heidi up a short flight of steps to a broad walkway that curved round the walls of what was an immense cavern, far above a floor filled with colossal versions of the now-familiar stone engine. Each was a disc some ten metres in diameter, with an intricate arrangement of cogwheels set into the surface like fossilised bones. A row of these engines snaked down the centre of the hall like the spine of a mythical monster.

The entire length of the walkway was lined with bystanders, clustered along the guard rail – the other guests invited for the ceremony. They were scientists, engineers, government officials, and Yaz was sure she spotted the past winner of a reality-TV show. As they awaited the grand switch-on, the audience was entertained by a full-size orchestra located on the hall floor, in the shadow of the stone engines.

'Is this the first time the system has gone live?' the Doctor asked Heidi.

'Apart from the test phase, yes.'

Yaz detected a note of hesitation in the other woman's voice. The Doctor had picked up on it too.

Heidi looked around, suddenly aware of the missing member of the party. 'Where is Captain von Trapp?'

'Gone to the little goatherd's room,' said Yaz.

'But that test phase was unusually short, wasn't it?' The Doctor pressed Heidi. 'There was one test three days ago, and then another today, and neither lasted more than a few seconds.'

Heidi frowned. 'How did you know . . .?'

Yaz was puzzled too. Judging from Heidi's reaction, the Doctor's assessment was right on the nose, but how could she possibly have known those details?

The Doctor gazed out over the generator hall, deep in thought. 'That's why I couldn't trace the source of the signal the first time – it wasn't around long enough to get a lock on. But that brief test still generated enough energy to kickstart an engine that had lain dormant aboard the TARDIS for years – and another at the heart of a Minotaur. Then today's test knocked out the TARDIS's own navigation systems.'

Yaz could see that the Doctor's pronouncement had confused Heidi, but it was slowly making sense to Yaz. Whatever was going on here, under the mountain, was inextricably linked to the stone engine Ryan had found in the coat pocket belonging to the Doctor's previous regeneration, and the one in the Minotaur. Her mind leaped to a terrible conclusion. The first engine had overloaded and then exploded. Had it not been for the muting effect of the TARDIS, which weakened the blast, it would've caused catastrophic destruction. And the Minotaur heart was only prevented from detonating by the Doctor's quick actions. Neither of those engines had been bigger than a large coin. With a feeling of dread, Yaz looked out over the supersized versions ranked together in the generator hall.

What would happen if these ones blew up?

As she pondered the question, a small, fast-moving shape emerged from the shadows at the far end of the cavernous hall. As it drew closer, Yaz saw that it was Penelope's robotic owl. Flying down the centre of the room, skimming the tops of the great stone engines, Yaz couldn't help thinking that it looked like a dark, winged omen.

15. The Clinic

Graham was lost. The colour-coded tunnels were all very well, but an actual map would've been useful. Following Heidi's example, he had touched his augmented name badge to the self-driving buggy's console, then instructed it to take him to the clinic. For the first part of the journey, all had gone as expected. It was only as the green tunnels gave way to purple, not red, that he realised he was off track. Maybe the buggy's speech-recognition software was, well, buggy. Or maybe it didn't understand his accent. Parked against one wall of the tunnel, he tried again, enunciating each syllable with exquisite care.

'*Cli-nic.*' Nothing. He tried again. '*Med-i-cal wing. Hos-pi-tal.*' He paused, then added, 'Please.' He knew it was a machine, but it couldn't hurt to be polite.

'Fault detected,' squawked the vehicle. 'Immediate maintenance required.' With that, it set off again at a brisk pace, the sudden acceleration throwing him back into the seat.

The car drew up to what appeared to be the main depot for the fleet of electric vehicles that served the power plant. Around the cavernous room were parked ranks of similar buggies, while others received attention from automated servicing systems. Graham's ride rolled to a stop and, when it was clear that it was taking him no further, he got out. Taking a closer look around, he realised that this place was more than a buggy depot. At the far end was a selection of road-going vehicles. With their swooping body-work and sleek profiles, he figured them for prototypes – the sort of automotive sculptures that manufacturers turn up with at international motor shows to show off their vision of the future. Clearly the Polichroniadis siblings were interested in a wide range of applications for their magical engine – it could power phones, power plants and even vehicles. He was pleased to see, parked among the SUVs and low-slung sports cars, the distinctive form of a double-decker bus. It looked like a Routemaster that had arrived from the future, after falling through a wormhole in time. Maybe it was.

Tearing himself away from the enticing sight, he commandeered another buggy and resumed his journey. As it threaded its way through the tunnels, he was comforted in the knowledge that at least there were no Minotaurs to contend with down here. He immediately regretted allowing that thought to cross his mind. Now, as he passed every shadowy tunnel, he expected one of the bronze monsters to be lurking there, ready to jump out at him.

'Come on, Graham. Pull yourself together.'

After years and years on the buses, he'd pictured a quiet retirement living alongside the love of his life, Ryan's grandma, Grace. He heaved a sigh at her memory. What he could never have envisaged was spending his latter years aboard the TARDIS with the Doctor, helping her to secure the secret in Vault 13, outwit a Minotaur or sneak around inside a Swiss mountain searching for his abducted grandson. At least he could enjoy a sit-down for now. Most of the time, there was a lot of running around, which was fine if you were thirty years younger, like Yaz and Ryan. Graham wasn't sure how much more of this 'saving the universe' business he had left in him. But, so long as Ryan needed him, he would put up with the constant terror and the frankly unnecessary levels of excitement.

So distracted by thoughts of Grace and home was he that he only noticed the lighting in the tunnels had turned from purple to red when the buggy came to a stop at a junction. On the wall next to him was a sign showing a symbol of a pair of serpents entwined round a winged staff. Graham recognised it as the ancient Greek symbol associated with medicine. Either that or . . . Graham tucked the cuffs of his trousers into his socks. Better safe than sorry. He left the buggy behind and set off on foot, arriving soon at an empty waiting area.

There was a curved reception desk, several rows of chairs, and a straggly potted plant that looked miserable from living underground. Calming music drifted out of invisible speakers, the soothing tone at odds with the selection of alarming posters on the walls – each featured a message on workplace safety, illustrated by a range of human limbs at risk of being chopped or crushed by heavy machinery. Beyond the desk, Graham could see down the length of a corridor lined with doors, presumably leading to examination rooms or wards. Staff in medical scrubs ducked in and out, studying charts or deep in conversation.

Graham wasn't sure how big this place was, but since it served the entire power plant it had to be a sizeable operation. That was a problem. He didn't have time to wander around, hoping to bump into Ryan. He needed to locate his grandson quickly, before his own absence was noted. No one was on duty at the desk, so he hurried to the other side, hoping to use his badge to access the clinic's computer files for information on his grandson. But, as he approached, he was stopped in his tracks by a disembodied voice.

'Welcome,' it said. 'Please touch the screen and state your medical emergency.'

A monitor was affixed to the front of the desk. It flashed up a list of options, ranging from 'the sniffles' to 'sucking chest wound', and left a space for a handprint ID. If Graham placed his palm against it, though, the system would recognise him for the intruder he was. Ignoring the computerised voice, he marched round the desk and touched his badge to the reader he found there. He held his breath for what felt like an age.

'Access granted, Panos Polichroniadis,' cooed the voice.

This was better than he could've hoped for. The Doctor had boosted his security level right up to the top – the system thought he was the boss.

'Please state your request.'

'Locate patient Ryan Sinclair.'

It hummed for a second, then spat out the answer. 'Talos Ward. Room AA94.' Along with the location, the screen displayed a map, showing the winding route to the ward. Graham committed the map to memory – his years as a bus driver ensured that remembering routes was easy for him. Then, retrieving his security pass, he slipped out of the waiting area and ambled along the corridor. He figured that 'ambling' was the least suspicious style of walking he could adopt. It suggested to any curious observer that he belonged there. However, it would take him some time to reach his destination at this relaxed pace. He had barely covered any distance when he passed the open door of a store cupboard. An idea flashed through his mind when he spotted a rack of white coats hanging up inside.

Feeling rather like Doctor Goldilocks, he tried several before finding one that fitted just right. For good measure, he snagged a clipboard, and his disguise was complete. Head buried in imaginary patient notes, he resumed his path to the ward. Now ambling was out – he could walk with purpose. He bluffed his way past the medical staff, passing unchallenged through bustling corridors, which gave way to emptier ones. He rounded a corner to be met by what looked like a bank-vault door. It was circular, about three metres in diameter and constructed from shining steel.

Closing his eyes, he pictured the map again, making sure he hadn't taken a wrong turn. But this was the place all right – and this was where the helpful route map ran out. Hoping that his all-access security pass would do the job one more time, he touched it to the reader by the side of the door. Too late, he noticed a discreet camera tucked into one corner of the ceiling, eyeing him from above. He had to assume he'd been spotted, which meant once inside he had to work quickly, before some big guy in a uniform tapped him on the shoulder and asked what he was doing on the premises. The heavy door ground open with painful slowness. He waited for it to clear the frame, then squeezed through the gap, noticing as he did so that the door had to be half a metre thick. Why did a hospital ward need such a formidable security measure?

The room on the other side was octagonal, with a branching corridor springing from each of its eight sides. According to Graham's information, Ryan was in room AA94. But down which corridor?

In the centre of the room was a nurse's station comprised of a wraparound desk inset with monitors. Graham's luck was holding, as the station was unattended. But, even as he scooted behind the desk, he could hear footsteps from along one of the corridors. Someone was coming. He needed to work fast. He looked back at the monitor, and was startled by what he saw. The screens displayed live images of the interiors of patients' rooms, along with constantly updated information regarding their vital signs. But that wasn't what grabbed his attention. Every hospital room he'd ever seen featured a bed, a telly and a bunch of grapes. These did not.

Instead, each contained a golden sarcophagus.

'Hello, Doctor.'

'No, I'm not the Doc–' He caught sight of his white coat and remembered. 'How can I help?'

A dour bespectacled man in a nurse's uniform thrust a clipboard at him. 'You must sign off on these charts.'

'Sure, no problem.' Graham said, his voice a little squeaky.

The numbers swam before him like his last maths exam. Which he'd failed.

'They look great. Great charts. Good work,' he said, scribbling an indecipherable signature at the foot of the page and getting rid of it as if it was burning him.

The nurse surveyed him narrowly. 'You are new.'

He nodded anxiously, feeling sweat prickle the back of his neck. 'Just transferred from . . . Holby City.'

The nurse sighed and turned away. 'This place gets through almost as many doctors as test subjects.'

Graham pretended to smile, but really he thought that didn't sound good. What nurse referred to their patients as 'test subjects'? What were they doing to Ryan in here?

The nurse bustled back down one of the corridors, leaving him alone at the monitoring station. Ryan was in one of those golden coffins, and it was up to Graham to get the poor boy out. He surveyed the array of screens. One was dedicated to a user interface, filled with a lot of buttons and controls with labels he didn't understand. This really wasn't his forte. He asked himself, *What would the Doctor do, if she was here?* The answer was obvious.

Push everything.

He clicked every button he could find.

There was a pause, then from all around the ward came a series of hisses, like a nest of vipers awakening at once. On the monitors he saw the door to every room slide back and every sarcophagus lid creak open.

He grinned. That was good.

An alarm began to sound, and a green light above the entrance to each corridor pulsed amber, then red.

That was less good.

What looked like steam was rising from each coffin; it poured over the rim to pool on the floor like marsh gas. Transfixed, he continued to watch the screen in horror as the occupants slowly began to stir. They rose stiffly from their coffins, and something about them made him decidedly uneasy. But he couldn't worry too much about them.

It was time to rescue Ryan.

With the alarm shrilling in his ears, he bolted down the corridor to room AA94, bursting in to find Ryan sitting upright in his open sarcophagus with a dazed expression. Graham's relief and delight at their reunion was tempered by Ryan's sallow appearance. The young man rubbed his arms, shivering violently. It was freezing in the room, colder than an open-topped bus ride through Sheffield in January.

'I feel awful,' Ryan muttered through chattering teeth.

'I've got a hot-water bottle in the TARDIS. Come on!'

Graham grabbed Ryan's hand and hauled him out of the coffin, half dragging him back into the corridor.

The doors were all wide open and each room they passed was ominously empty. All but one. A low moan came from inside. Bracing himself, Graham peered in. And there he was: a glowing man with matted hair and eyes like burning embers. He moved with sudden, jerky motions. A wave of heat rolled off him and around his body hung a shimmer – the sort of haze that Graham associated with hot tarmac roads.

'D'you feel that?' he said to Ryan.

They moved on quickly, grateful to leave the man behind, only to run into more just like him. Men and women lurched along the corridor, while even more were pouring out of the adjoining passageways that funnelled towards the nurse's station. All wore the same close-fitting bronze-coloured bodysuit, and all had the same pulsing eyes. Over the sound of the alarm came a howl – a deep animal wail of pain and fury. *Test subjects.* The phrase rung in Graham's head. Whatever had been done to these poor souls had driven them out of their minds.

The nurse came racing along the corridor. He rounded on Graham with a mixture of fury and terror. 'What have you done?'

'What have I done? What have *you* done to these people?'

'The doors!' said Ryan.

Steel shutters were descending from the ceiling at the entrance to each corridor, and the main vault door was swinging shut.

'It's an automatic lockdown,' said the nurse. 'In case of a breach.'

At the sound of their voices, all the bronze figures suddenly grew still, and then in a single movement turned towards the trio.

Graham sighed. From Kerblam to the planet Desolation, Pendle Hill to Alabama, why did it always come to this?

'RUN!' he yelled.

The nurse took off first, while Graham pulled the injured Ryan along beside him. They threaded their way past the clustering figures, and the bronze men and women grabbed out blindly, howling. The door gap was narrowing.

'I don't know if they're trying to hurt us,' said Graham, puffing loudly, out of breath. 'But, even if they don't mean to, they're red hot. Be careful!'

Granddad and grandson dodged this way and that to avoid the grasping hands. Graham yanked Ryan out of the path of one only to put himself in its way. The figure gripped his wrist and, for a brief moment, he was face-to-face with the unfortunate man. Something glittered in one unnatural eye. Graham glimpsed it for only a second, but even in that brief time he was certain of what he'd seen.

A cogwheel, exactly like the ones set into the stone engine.

There was a sharp smell and Graham felt a burning sting on his skin. The bronze figure's hand had burned all the way through his shirt. Shaking it off, Graham pressed on towards the exit and, with one last effort, heaved Ryan through the narrowing gap of the main door, hurling himself after him. He landed in a tangle of limbs on the floor outside, as the door clanged shut behind them.

He lifted his head to look around. There was no sign of the nurse. Graham had a sick feeling that he hadn't made it out. But others had. Distant shrieks and howls echoed back down the corridor. Many of the bronze figures had been trapped in the ward, but an unknown number had escaped and were loose in the power plant.

16. The Engines Cannae Take It

Penelope's drone owl perched on her shoulder. She and Panos occupied a separate section of the walkway, away from the crowds. *Like a royal box*, Yaz thought. It was positioned overlooking the centre of the generator hall, with the best view of the machinery. The mechanical dogs, Scylla and Charybdis, rebuilt and with a fresh lick of paint, stood guard on either side. The siblings' presence, although hardly unexpected, posed a problem.

Yaz cornered the Doctor as soon as she could. 'Panos and Penelope will recognise us. We need to keep our heads down and blend in. So, Doctor –' she chose her next words carefully, hoping not to offend her friend – 'try not to do anything, y'know, too Time Lord-y.'

Before the Doctor could object, Panos began to speak. Yaz noted that Penelope took a back seat while her brother beguiled the audience with a speech. He spoke eloquently about the future of Earth's energy supply, the search for a clean and sustainable solution, and how humbling it was that it should fall to him and his sister to be custodians of that solution. Even Yaz had to admit that he had some style. When the applause had died away, Panos announced that the moment had come to change the course of human history. In front of him was a podium topped with remote switchgear in the form of a large green button beneath a protective clear case.

'And, since we are talking about the future of humankind,' Panos said, 'it is only fitting that the honour of heralding the new dawn should fall to *our* future.'

At that, a young boy and girl, each no more than five years old, emerged from the audience. They wore the traditional outfits of their homelands: the boy in the costume of Greece, with its distinctive white kilt, sash and moccasins with pompoms; the girl in a colourful Austrian dirndl. A great 'aww' went up from the guests at the sight of the impossibly cute youngsters. But, as the beaming pair walked hand-in-hand towards Panos, they were overtaken by another figure.

''Scuse me, coming through.'

The Doctor shot out of the crowd and narrowly avoided trampling the children under her big boots as she marched along the walkway to confront Panos and Penelope. A murmur of disquiet rippled through the audience. The children started to cry. Yaz placed a palm to her face, unable to watch. So much for keeping a low profile.

'You!' Panos's charming mask slipped as he recognised her.

Scylla and Charybdis growled at her approach, straining to reach the individual who had offended their master. Panos commanded them to heel.

'Something's been bothering me since I got here,' the Doctor said. 'You call this a generator hall, but those aren't turbines. You're not burning coal or gas. There's no hydroelectric supply, and if it's nuclear then I can't see it – unless you're using one of those teeny-weeny portable barbecue reactors from the twenty-fifth century. Which you aren't.' She paused. 'So, the question is, if you're not generating the power here, then where's it coming from?'

Panos said nothing. Uncharacteristically, he seemed lost for words. He shuffled his feet and responded to the question only with a smile. Yaz could see it was forced, for the benefit of the gathered guests.

'You don't know?' The Doctor gawped.

Some of the audience were growing perturbed. A ripple of doubt swept through the room.

'You plan to just switch this thing on and cross your fingers?' the Doctor continued. 'That's so far beyond reckless, there isn't a word for it in any Earth language.'

'Doctor, please, you're upsetting my guests.' Panos found his tongue. 'Allow me to enlighten you.'

'Go on then.' The Doctor folded her arms. 'I've had to endure years of Cybermansplaining. I can handle this.'

Perhaps sensing the mood in the room turning against him, Panos stepped to the edge of the walkway and indicated the great rank of engines. 'What you are looking at is the Aénaos Engine, a device that produces power indefinitely without the need for an energy source.'

'A perpetual-motion machine?' The Doctor was incredulous. 'You can't really believe that, can you? It breaks the laws of physics. Even Time Lord physics. The universe doesn't allow such a thing.'

Panos dismissed her objections with a wave. 'Nevertheless, a scaled-down version of this same device has been running safely in my mobile phones for years.'

'Yeah, the same harmless device that's powering a killer Minotaur statue still going strong after four thousand years.'

Panos's expression darkened. He did not like being made to look a fool, especially at what he had expected to be his shining moment of triumph. 'If you're so certain,' he said, 'then tell me exactly what it is, Doctor.'

The Doctor frowned. 'Can't. Yet. Unlike you, I want to be sure before I start jumping to conclusions.'

'The world cannot wait for your answer. The ice caps are melting, the seas are rising and full of junk. We're belching out billions of tonnes of carbon dioxide into the atmosphere. When the Aénaos Engine goes live, that will be the moment when science says, "Enough." The moment when the human race begins to reverse the effects of hundreds of years of wasteful living. I'm saving the planet. Right now.'

'It's a remote switch,' the Doctor quietly informed Yaz, who had arrived at her side a moment or two earlier. 'The main controls must be close by.'

Ten metres above the walkway, technicians crowded a long viewing-window. Yaz could discern the outline of equipment. 'There!'

Panos flipped up the case covering the green button.

'I may be able to interrupt the activation signal.' The Doctor's hand flashed like a Wild West gunslinger's, dipping into her pocket for – Yaz realised too late – her sonic screwdriver. With the right setting, she could have cut the signal between the remote switching gear and the engines, and at least delay the switch-on. But the Doctor's face fell as she felt around inside her empty pocket, forgetting that she'd been forced to give up her sonic at the door.

Panos depressed the button.

Nothing happened for several seconds and then, with a terrible grinding like the sound of clashing tectonic plates, the giant mechanism began to move. Yaz was aware of the slightest of tremors, as if the entire mountain had shifted minutely. Not sure if she had imagined it, Yaz glanced at the Doctor to see if she'd noticed it too, but she was staring at the Aénaos Engine. There was another tremor, more violent this time, which caused Yaz to stumble. Small cries of alarm erupted from the guests as they lost their footing. The orchestra played on, the vibration causing their instruments to produce unsettling notes in a dread symphony. Listening to them, Yaz was reminded of the band that continued playing aboard the stricken *Titanic* even as it sank. Looking up, she saw that the cave walls of the generator hall were pulsating. Yaz met the Doctor's eye; she'd definitely noticed now. Small fragments of rock in the roof, loosened by the vibrations, began to rain down on the guests below, pattering against the walkway like hail. A larger rock broke off and flew downwards, missing the crowd but smashing a hole through the walkway. Alarm turned to panic.

At the first tremor, Panos and Penelope had left the royal box and made their way up a flight of steps to the control room. At the long viewing-window, Yaz could see technicians charging back and forth in disarray.

The Doctor's boots rang off the metal steps as she gave chase. Yaz followed her. They slipped inside the control room unchallenged amid the chaos that the switch-on had unleashed. Panos was in discussion with an engineer. Over the hooting of alarm klaxons, Yaz could make out the technician's flustered words.

'. . . unprecedented readings. Way above all of our projections, Mr Polichroniadis.'

There was another rumble in the mountain and the floor beneath them shook.

'You have to switch it off!' called the Doctor. 'It's only going to get worse.'

'No,' insisted Panos, his violet eyes cruel and resolute.

'Panos,' Penelope said quietly, 'maybe we should listen to her.'

Her brother cast her a hurt look.

There was a growl and a crash as though the gates of the underworld itself were cracking open and Cerberus, the three-headed guard dog of Hell, was on its way. Even Panos's gleaming smile faltered. At his side, Penelope continued to appeal to him in vain.

'If you're not going to do it, then I will.' Taking charge, the Doctor moved to the main control panel.

'Stop her!' Panos commanded.

'No!' Penelope stood blocking his way.

Yaz noted the expression on Panos's face. She had never seen anyone look more betrayed.

The engineer stood frozen over the control panel. The board was awash with flashing warning lights. 'The energy signal is increasing! The system cannot cope with this much power. It's going to overload.'

'What about the automatic shutdown?' asked the Doctor calmly.

The engineer shook his head. 'Failed. And all three redundant systems.'

'Talk me through the manual override,' said the Doctor.

'It's no use,' replied the engineer.

For the first time, Yaz detected a crack in Panos's self-assured demeanour. A sheen of sweat coated his brow. Even he looked worried.

The Doctor stared from the viewing-window. Above the massive Aénaos Engine, the air shimmered and warped. For a second, the entire mechanism seemed to vanish, but even as Yaz formed the thought in her head it was back again, solid as rock.

'Oh no,' said the Doctor, observing with quiet trepidation. 'I know where the power's coming from.'

There was another shudder, and then a new sound. Yaz felt it before she heard it. A tick, but not like any she had ever heard. It was the tick of the first clock, the tick that set the universe going.

It made her teeth ache in their gums and the back of her skull feel like something was drilling into it. Glancing around the control room, she saw that the technicians were clutching their heads, some writhing on the floor and crying in pain, Panos and Penelope among them. Through the window, below on the walkway, the guests were in the same distressed state. Even the Doctor had succumbed to the effects of the terrible sound. Yaz screwed up her eyes at the throbbing pain and tried not to black out.

And then, as quickly as it started, it faded away until it was no more than the tick of a grandfather clock in an old house at the end of a dusty corridor. As Yaz opened her eyes, she saw that the others around her were sitting up and blinking, bewildered. The mountain was still.

'What are the readings?' called Panos, struggling to his feet.

'They've stabilised,' came the mystified voice of the chief engineer. 'They look ... good.' The surprise and relief in his voice was palpable. 'Higher than our projections, but they've levelled off.'

Panos spun round to confront the Doctor. 'See. It's a success. A glorious success. Feel free to stay and enjoy the champagne.'

The Doctor stared at him, aghast. 'This engine of yours is going to blow. In ten minutes, or ten hours, or ten days. And, when it does, it will not only take this mountain with it, but the entire planet too.' The room fell silent, the technicians cowed by her prediction. 'Have a lovely party, though.'

She nodded to Yaz and the two of them headed for the exit. 'We can't shut the engine down from here without setting it off, but we might be able to do something about it at the other end – where it's drawing all that power from.'

'And where's that, exactly?'

'I have an idea, but let's find out for sure.'

As they reached the door, their guide, Heidi, ran inside and urgently addressed Panos.

'Sir, there's a problem.'

'What now?' he snapped in exasperation.

'A security breach in the Talos ward. And . . .' She hesitated, awkwardly aware that everyone in the room was staring at her. 'Someone has stolen a bus.'

The Doctor and Yaz exchanged a look.

'Graham,' they said together.

17. The Winged Pegabus

The speeding electric bus was a near-silent streak of metallic red in the dim tunnel. At the wheel Graham steered it round another bend and grinned. His choice of getaway vehicle had been extensive. He could've picked anything from that showroom of exotic prototypes – a sports car, an SUV or a saloon – but there had been no question in his mind about which would do the job most effectively. From a practical point of view, he needed something that could fit everyone, so that ruled out the sports car. It also had to be unstoppable, and since Panos didn't have a tank, the bus had been the only logical choice. Though, if he was honest, the decision wasn't all about using his head; his heart had steered him too. It was the most glorious bus he'd ever set eyes on, let alone driven. He disengaged the autonomous driving function and returned the vehicle to manual control – he wasn't going to pass up driving this bus himself.

The tunnels were designed to accommodate the bus's dimensions, so the ceiling-height clearance wasn't a problem, but as he'd got to grips with the bends he'd collected a few lights from the walls. They were draped around the bus like Christmas decorations. There was a sudden crash and a tinkle of glass. There went a another.

From the first row of seats behind him came a groan.

'How're you doing, son?'

'I'd like to get off now,' said a weak voice.

Graham risked a glance at Ryan. His face was flushed and his T-shirt soaked with sweat. In fact, as Graham looked, it seemed that steam was rising off Ryan's shirt. This was no ordinary fever. If Graham had to guess, Ryan was nearly as hot as the burning people they'd left behind in the tunnel.

The walls shook. But this time it wasn't his doing. Had to be the Doctor and Yaz in the main generator hall. He was on his way there now and, with a bit of luck, he'd arrive before the burning people caught up. Graham still wasn't sure whether the unfortunate test subjects intended them any harm, but he wasn't planning on hanging around long enough to find out.

The vibration continued, causing splinters of stone to fall from the roof and spray against the windscreen. He switched on the wipers. As they cleared his view, powerful LED headlights picked out a large rock directly in their path. He wrenched the wheel, guiding the bus round the obstacle, but the tunnel wasn't quite wide enough and one wheel clipped the rock. There was the crunch of buckling metal and the bus lurched from side to side. With calm steering, Graham got it under control again, steadying the vehicle. He patted the rim of the wheel.

'Good lad.'

'Hmm?' Ryan sat up.

'Not you, lad.'

Ryan lay back down again with a confused expression.

The bus shot into a new section of the tunnels. Graham noted with relief that this section was illuminated by green lights. 'Stay with me. We're almost there.'

One more bend and then a long, straight run and the entrance to the main generator hall was in sight. Two figures waited at the side of the tunnel. On seeing the red bus careering towards them, one stuck out her thumb in the universal hitch-hiker's signal. Graham slammed on the brakes and came to a stop. He slapped the door controls and they hissed open.

Yaz hopped on. 'Two to Bramall Lane, please.'

The Doctor paused for a second, one foot on the step. She looked back, an interested frown crossing her features. 'What's that?'

A ghastly howling and the thundering of footsteps echoed along the tunnel.

Glancing in the wing mirror, Graham saw dozens of figures shambling out of the darkness. The burning people he and Ryan had set free from the clinic were lurching towards them.

'Graham,' said the Doctor, 'did you accidentally unleash a zombie horde?'

Without waiting for an answer, she bounded on and he stamped on the accelerator. The motor delivered a massive shove and the bus leaped forward. They were on their way again.

Seeing Ryan lying prostrate across the front seats, Yaz crossed quickly to his side. The Doctor joined her, but not before throwing a questioning look at Graham. He was about to say something, when she interrupted.

'Tell me later. Concentrate on getting us out of here first.'

He nodded and focused on the task. The three-kilometre route was clear in his mind – all he had to do was drive it. Soon he had outdistanced the burning people and they were no more than an unsettling glow in the rear-view mirror. But, just as Graham felt himself relax, the Doctor's voice brought him back to reality.

'How fast can this thing go?' she called from the back of the bus, where she was gazing out of the window.

Graham glanced at the speedometer. It was a heads-up display, the kind you got in fighter jets and, these days, high-end German cars. 'We're doing forty – that's pretty quick for a near-dark barely-big-enough tunnel bored through an alp. Why d'you ask?'

'Old friends,' said the Doctor.

Graham raised his eyes to the rear-view mirror again. Like everything in the bus, it was state of the art – instead of an old-fashioned reflecting mirror, it was a digital screen fed by a camera built into the rear of the bus, and displayed a perfect one hundred and eighty degree field of view. It was currently showing, in crystal-clear high definition, the images of Scylla and Charybdis bounding after them. The headless robot hounds tore through the tunnel, eating up the distance between them, the beady lasers of their optical range-finders gleaming in the darkness.

'Why did I ask?' Graham mumbled.

The Doctor pulled a panel off the bus interior and began digging around in some kind of fuse box.

Graham concentrated on the tunnel in front of them. The headlights flooded it with a cool white glow. What he could see was perfectly straight, but at any second there could be an unexpected corner, and if he entered it too quickly he knew he would struggle to make the turn. However, the alternative was to risk being caught by those monstrosities. He pressed down on the accelerator, summoning more power from the electric motor. It responded with a surge of speed. The heads-up display ticked from forty to fifty. He risked another glance in the mirror and instantly regretted it. He snapped his attention back to the route as the headlights revealed a sharp turn in the tunnel ahead. Hit the brakes or hit the rock wall – that was his only choice. He waited till the last possible second, stamped on the brake pedal and swung the wheel. For a bus, it cornered like a Ferrari.

There was a sound of wrenching metal, and for a moment he thought they had hit another obstacle. Then he realised it was coming from the back of the bus: one of the dogs had caught them and clamped on to the back end. There was a series of tearing sounds as its razor-sharp claws bit into the bodywork. The dog hauled itself on to the roof of the bus and out of sight of the camera. Graham winced as he heard it scuttle along the roof. There was an emergency hatch above the driver's compartment – a perfect way to gain access.

It was coming for him.

They'd cleared the bend.

'Everyone, hold on!'

Graham mashed the accelerator pedal and spun the steering wheel. The back of the bus swung out, clipping the wall of the tunnel. The force was enough to loosen the robotic dog's grip on the roof. It was thrown off, but didn't fall, instead managing to cling on with two of its legs. It hung down outside the driver's compartment, separated from Graham by only a thin layer of aluminium and a glass window. This close, he could hear its terrible growl.

The Doctor was at his side. 'Open the window!'

'No way! Are you crazy?'

'Do it, Graham. Trust me.'

Against his better judgement, he tapped the switch and with a hum the window rolled down into the doorframe.

'Fetch!' shouted the Doctor, tossing out what looked like a short metal post, wound with wires and blinking lights. It flew past the dog and bounced along the tunnel floor.

There was a brief fire of sparks as the robotic dog immediately detached its claws and jumped after the object. In the gloom, Graham could see Scylla and Charybdis wrestling over it.

'Electronic bone,' said the Doctor. 'Digitally irresistible.'

Graham gazed at her in awe. So that's what she'd been doing in the fuse box.

'Look!' shouted Yaz.

The unmistakable bright blur of daylight filled the end of the tunnel. Graham pressed ahead and a minute later they emerged, blinking, into the glare of a sunny alpine afternoon.

And heading straight for a precipice.

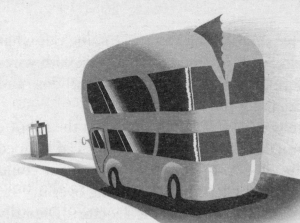

18. Left. Right?

Graham braked, bringing the bus to a stop centimetres before what seemed like a flimsy crash barrier. From his high-seated vantage, he could see the road descending steeply for several thousand metres in a series of serpentine bends that wound through patches of melting snow. Here and there along the route, crash barriers were broken or bowed, evidence of previous mishaps. Every drop was straight down. He surveyed the road with a shudder.

Ryan let out a moan and writhed in his seat. Yaz tended to him as best she could, but Graham knew that his grandson was in great peril.

'Panos is not going to give up,' he said. 'He needs Ryan. He won't let him get away.'

As he said it, he caught sight of a movement out of the corner of his eye. A winged shadow swept down over the mountain.

'Penelope's owl,' said Yaz.

The Doctor's electronic bone may have stalled the pursuing dogs, but they weren't the only predators in the Polichroniadises' zoo of horrors.

'We'll be safe in the TARDIS,' said the Doctor. 'But you have to get us down this mountain.'

Graham floored it as the owl swooped low over the bus. He went out wide to take the first hairpin bend and wished he'd chosen a sports car after all.

The bus had to follow a zigzag course, while the drone owl could fly a straight path. However, to their puzzlement, the bird kept its distance, hovering a little way behind and above them.

'Why isn't it attacking?' the Doctor mused. 'Those talons could do some serious damage.'

'Can we just be relieved for once that something isn't trying to kill us?' said Graham, guiding the bus round another bend. One misjudged turn, one unexpected patch of black ice, and it'd be the end of the road – in every sense.

The Doctor tapped her lip thoughtfully. 'Now, what are owls known for?'

'A love of pussy cats and an odd choice in boat paintwork?' suggested Yaz.

The Doctor snapped her fingers. 'Exceptionally good vision.' She leaned close to the window for a sight of the robotic bird. 'It's watching us.'

'Why?' asked Graham, wheeling the bus round to prepare for the next bend. He went to adjust the steering wheel, but as he did so it spun out of his hands in the opposite direction.

'Graham!' Yaz cried as the bus lurched towards the edge of the road and the drop.

'It's not me! I'm not steering!'

The Doctor's face was grim. 'The bus is being controlled remotely. The owl is sending back video to aid the driver.'

As she said it, the heads-up display flickered then vanished, and was replaced by an image of Panos. He was holding what looked like a video-game controller.

'Enjoying the ride?' He tilted the controller.

The bus mimicked the movement and swerved again, scraping the safety barrier. With a squeak of tyres and a shimmy, it straightened up again. Panos smiled. He was toying with them. The bus was under his control – at any moment he could stop it or send it over the edge.

'My people are waiting for you at the bottom of the road.' There was a series of clunks from the doors as they locked. 'That's in case you were thinking of disembarking,' he added. 'Ryan, my friend, I will see you soon.'

The bus continued its descent, now with the distant Panos at the wheel.

'If we're going to regain control,' whispered the Doctor, 'we need to jam his signal.'

'What about using your sonic?' hissed Graham.

'Confiscated,' she replied. 'But this bus is packed with more technology than the average Judoon battle-cruiser.' Dropping to her hands and knees, she removed another panel, this time next to the driver's compartment. 'I can use the bus as the battery and your phones as antennae. Now I just need an oscillator.' She began pulling out handfuls of wiring and circuit boards. Soon she was up to her shoulders inside the compartment. With a quiet but triumphant 'Ah-ha!' she re-emerged, covered in a spaghetti-like tangle of wires, holding a circuit board and eyeing its various elements. 'Right, this'll do as the inductor. A couple of capacitors and we're good to go.'

Graham remained in the driver's seat, even though he was not currently *in* the driver's seat. They had been halfway down the mountain when Panos hijacked the controls. At least being a passenger gave Graham time to admire the scenery. The lower slopes were covered with fir trees and below them, at the edge of the forest, lay the village from which they'd set off earlier that day. But now the bad guys were waiting there, unless the Doctor did something fast.

'Ready!' she said, leaping up. Wires trailed from the dashboard to the circuit board clutched in her hands, then on into the two remaining Aénaos phones. The Doctor joined a couple of metal connectors, and there was a flash and a hum. On the heads-up display, the image of Panos wavered.

'What's going on?' He prodded his controller in confusion and frowned when the bus didn't respond.

'Sorry, that was me,' said the Doctor.

'What have you done?' Panos was barely holding his fury in check.

'That's not important. What matters is that I'm going offline for a bit. I need to check something out.' She adjusted a component on the circuit board and his furious image faded out in a flurry of interference. 'Try not to blow up the world while I'm away.' She glanced at Graham. 'What're you waiting for? Drive!'

Graham dispatched the last few bends in a matter of minutes and soon they were on the final stretch, heading towards the village. Almost home free. But, as they crested a low rise, they were met by the sight of two black SUVs straddling the road. Taking cover behind them, Panos's security team aimed their weapons at the oncoming bus.

'Any ideas?' Graham eased off the accelerator, unsure of their next move. Beyond the roadblock lay the sanctuary of the TARDIS, but right now it seemed a long way off.

The Doctor fished out the TARDIS key from where it hung on the chain round her neck. 'I can open it from here.'

Yaz's eyes met Graham's in a look of mutual confusion. 'Yes, but once we stop the bus,' she said to the Doctor, 'we'll have to get off while carrying Ryan, then cross open ground to the TARDIS. We'd never make it.'

'We don't *have* to stop,' said the Doctor.

'What, just drive in?' said Yaz.

Graham shook his head doubtfully. 'Uh, Doc, aren't you forgetting something? Big bus, *little* doorway.'

'Don't you worry about the dimensions,' said the Doctor with a grin. 'The TARDIS'll take care of that.'

'I hope you know what you're doing,' Graham muttered, gripping the steering wheel with sweaty palms and pressing down on the accelerator.

There were pops of gunfire as the security team tried to halt them. Graham felt the bus list – the shooters must've hit one of the tyres – but momentum kept it moving forward at speed. Sensing that their target wasn't about to stop, the security team dived out of its path, just as the bus ploughed through the parked SUVs, knocking them aside like skittles. The remains of the shot-out tyre flew off the wheel and the steel rim hit the asphalt, trailing sparks. The bus slewed off course. Graham calmly adjusted the steering, bringing the nose to point at the police box. He glanced at the Doctor's face. She had a smile like the Mona Lisa's, except more infuriatingly unknowable.

'Doctor?'

'Open sesame.'

The TARDIS door popped open.

Sure, Graham knew that it was bigger on the inside, but they were *outside*.

Nope. Nothing this large could fit through a gap that small.

He screwed his eyes tight shut. 'Nope, nope, nope.'

'Graham, BRAKE!'

Reacting to the Doctor's voice, he slammed his foot down. The brakes bit and the bus pulled up like a lassoed mustang. He opened his eyes and blinked.

They were inside the TARDIS. They'd made it!

But this wasn't the console room.

It reminded him of the underground garage he'd seen briefly in the Polichroniadises' London house. However, the Doctor's taste differed from the billionaires'. Arranged on the showroom-white floor here were just three vehicles: a canary-yellow vintage roadster with the number-plate WHO 1, a white manta-ray-shaped vehicle that appeared to be half hovercraft, half road car, and –

'Is that a Mark One Ford Capri?'

Graham spun round at the sound of Ryan's rejuvenated voice. The boy still looked worn out, but he sounded better than he had in ages. It was probably being back aboard the TARDIS, Graham decided. The ship was protective of its crew.

The Doctor nodded. 'Mint condition, two thousand miles, thirteen careful owners.'

She and Graham began to help Ryan off the bus, each taking an arm. Yaz was about to follow when she heard her phone ring in her pocket. Leaving the others to head off without her, she answered the call.

'Yaz, it's me.'

The voice was distinctive. There could be no question about who was on the other end.

'Doctor?'

'Now, listen carefully . . .'

This made no sense. Yaz could see the Doctor from here, walking past the yellow roadster with Ryan and Graham, and she wasn't holding a phone.

'Who is this?'

'You know who. I'm calling from the future and I don't know how long I've got. This sort of thing only works so long as the paradox machine is functioning.'

'Paradox what?'

'You don't know about that yet? You will very soon. Are you alone?'

Yaz was sure the others were out of earshot. 'Uh, yeah.'

'Good. I don't want past me suspecting anything. If she finds out we've spoken, she's likely to do something different in her future – my past – which will mess up your timeline. You know what she's like. Yaz, it is vital she doesn't learn that we've spoken. Understood?'

'Not really, but okay.'

'So, when the time comes – and you'll know when it does – it's left, *right*? Hang on.' There was a pause. 'Yeah, double-checked and that's right. *Left*. Just to be clear, that's right as in "okay", not right as in "turn right". Do not, under any circumstances, turn right.'

'Right. I mean … yes. Got it.' This was definitely the weirdest conversation Yaz had ever had. It was her Doctor, but not now. *Then*. She wasn't Doctor Now; she was Doctor Then. Which meant there was one thing Yaz had to ask. 'So, if you're calling from the future, does that mean everything works out and the world doesn't explode?'

'That entirely depends,' said Doctor Then evenly, 'on how well you can follow instructions.'

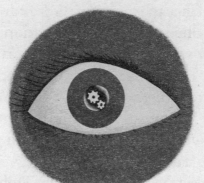

19. The Souvlaki Gambit

Still dazed from the conversation, Yaz joined the Doctor in the console room. She was alone. Yaz saw by the rise and fall of the time-rotor that they were already underway. The Doctor wasn't wasting a moment. There she stood over the controls, unaware of the call from Doctor Then or her future self's instruction not to share it with Doctor Now. Yaz could feel a blush rise to her cheeks – she felt as though she was cheating on her. With her.

'You okay?' asked the Doctor.

'Nothing. I mean, yes. I'm fine. How are you?'

The Doctor's features curled into a question. 'Who were you talking to?'

Oh no. She must've seen Yaz answer the call on the bus. 'No one,' Yaz snapped, then repeated it with an affectedly casual air. 'No one.'

The Doctor waggled her eyebrows. 'A special friend?'

'Definitely not. No one special.' Yaz changed the subject. 'How's Ryan?'

'Graham's taken him to the sick-bay. I say "sick-bay", but it's more of a cupboard. Told him he should check the expiry dates on the medicine bottles before he gives Ryan anything – there's stuff in there from before the Cretaceous period.'

'Any idea what's wrong with Ryan?'

'Not yet, but I'm sure it's connected to those stone engines.'

The time-rotor slowed to a stop and the *vworp* of the TARDIS's dematerialisation procedure filled the console room. There was a thud as the timeship settled.

'We're here,' said the Doctor, swiping the door controls.

'And where is here, exactly?'

The exterior door swung open and the Doctor headed outside. 'Once the Aénaos Engine was switched on under the mountain, it started to draw power at a tremendous rate. I was able to lock on to the energy signal and follow it to the source.'

They emerged from the TARDIS on to the roof of a tall building in the middle of an unfamiliar city. Yaz looked out over the scene. Something was terribly wrong. Office blocks were overgrown with weeds, others had toppled over and were no more than piles of rubble. There were no cars or buses. Roads were cracked, trees grew at intersections, and the streets were empty of people. Save for the throaty caws of roosting crows on the building opposite, the city was deathly quiet. At various points along a river choked with sludge and rusting boats were the crumbling remains of bridges. Following the path of the river, Yaz's eye fell on a dome-shaped building and she felt her heart hammer in her chest. She recognised it.

'St Paul's Cathedral.' She grabbed the Doctor. 'This is London.'

'I'm afraid so. A hundred years on from the day we left.'

All of this devastation had been caused in a mere century. 'What happened?'

'The Aénaos Engine,' said the Doctor. 'Under the mountain, when the generator was switched on, I saw something that made me suspect what was happening.'

Yaz's mind flashed back to the moment when the engine briefly vanished. 'I saw that too. It disappeared.'

'Phased in and out of time, to be exact. Remember Heidi told us that they'd tested the engine just before we arrived? That's what interfered with the TARDIS's navigation systems when we tried to land – a massive disruption in space–time. You see, the Aénaos Engine draws its power *across* time, effectively stealing it from Earth's own future.'

Yaz regarded the blasted landscape in shock as the full force of the Doctor's explanation hit home. Every drop of energy produced in the future had been sucked back in time to be consumed by the Aénaos Engine. Over the years, Yaz had experienced the occasional power cut and blackout, being forced to resort to a torch or light a candle for a few hours. But this was different. Earth had suffered a permanent blackout. Power was the planet's lifeblood – food, water, transport and communication all relied upon electricity, directly or indirectly. Losing all of it was unthinkable.

'Without power, society has broken down,' said the Doctor. 'And I've no doubt it's the same picture across the world. The end of civilisation as you know it.' She smiled bitterly. 'But, for the people of Earth in Panos's time, it will seem as if their dream of clean, sustainable energy has been granted. What they don't know is that they're taking it from the future of their own children and grandchildren.'

Yaz clapped her hands to her head, as if trying to prevent her brain from exploding. 'But, if that's already happened, then we're in a future that can't exist! We can't be here, but we are. That's –'

'A strange and chewy concept,' finished the Doctor with a grin. 'A paradox, if you like. The Aénaos Engine is what we in the time-travel biz call a paradox machine. And this is what often happens when people – the Nimons, Panos and Penelope – dabble with time-travel technology. It's part of a Time Lord's job to prevent such machines from being built, or to untangle the mess they create when they are.'

'So can we stop it from happening?' said Yaz. 'Change the future?'

The Doctor offered an uncertain nod. 'This future isn't set. It *can* be altered. But, if we don't manage to switch off the Aénaos Engine before it explodes, that doesn't really matter, since there won't be *any* future.'

There was the sound of hurried footsteps behind them.

'Doc, you gotta come quick.' Graham waited at the entrance to the TARDIS, his face pale with worry. 'Ryan's getting worse.'

They found Ryan in his room aboard the TARDIS, endlessly pacing up and down, muttering to himself. Waves of nervous energy rolled off him and the air around his body crackled with heat.

'Ryan?' said the Doctor softly.

'He can't hear you,' said Graham. 'Just keeps mumbling something about Talos. And, Doc, look at his eye.'

Ryan reached the far side of the room and, in his mania, turned briskly for yet another lap. He stared straight ahead, wide-eyed, but not seeing his friends. Against the ink-dark pupil, the outline of a cogwheel burned like hot coal.

'Doc, I think it's a piece of that stone engine we found in the TARDIS,' said Graham. 'And there's something else. Panos has got the same thing in his eye.'

Graham's words must have penetrated some conscious part of Ryan, as all at once he stopped walking and froze in the centre of the room.

Words tripping over themselves, he gabbled everything Penelope had told him about the Talos project.

'We need to get him to a surgeon,' said Yaz.

It was a little later. Following his frantic explanation, Ryan had resumed pacing his room. There seemed to be nothing anyone could do to still his restless energy. They left him there and gathered in the console room in order to plot their next move.

'No,' cautioned Graham. 'Ryan said they tried removing the cogwheel from some of their test subjects. Not one of them survived.'

'What about a surgeon from another planet?' Yaz persisted. 'Doctor, I bet you know someone – or something – who could do it.'

'I'm afraid not, Yaz. The fragment is not simply embedded in his body like a foreign object. It appears to have bonded with him, effectively turning Ryan into a human engine.' She frowned in thought. 'Which means it draws power from the future, just like the Aénaos Engine.' She snapped her fingers and spun round to face the others, her face shining with excitement. 'If we can cut off the flow of energy, then the engines will simply cease working. Without power, the Aénaos Engine can't overload, and removing that fragment from Ryan will be like taking out a stray eyelash.'

The Doctor activated the ship's viewscreen along the wall beside the console.

'Great, Doc,' said Graham, 'but how do we pull the plug on all that power?'

'That's exactly what we do, Graham. Trick is finding the plug.' On the screen was some kind of map. 'It's a geographical, astronomical and chronological plot of our recent journey in space and time,' explained the Doctor. She indicated a section on the far left of the map. 'This is the mountain containing the Aénaos Engine – our departure point.' She traced a wavy yellow line that sprang from their origin and arced across the years and miles of the map. 'And this is the energy signal the TARDIS followed one hundred years into Earth's future.' She tapped the end of the line. 'To this point – where we are now.'

Yaz studied the route. 'The line isn't straight. It takes a detour. See, here.' Shortly after leaving the Aénaos Engine, the line altered course, passing through a waypoint.

'Good spot, Yaz,' said the Doctor, examining the kink in the energy signal's path. 'Now, why would all that power be routeing through here, hmm? Let's find out what you are.' She turned to the console and programmed the navigation system with the co-ordinates. 'Interesting,' she said, reacting to the location of their next hop. 'What's your feeling on souvlaki?'

Graham frowned. 'Is that one of those Venusian martial arts you're always going on about?'

The Doctor looked up from the console. 'No, Graham, it's meat on a stick.' She slapped a switch and stamped on a pedal, sending the TARDIS once more into the time-vortex. They were on their way.

20. The Fires of Talos

Island of Crete, circa 2000 BC

Icarus's face flickered with firelight as he emerged from the dim skyship into the bright sunshine of the morning. Flames from his torch bent and snapped in the freshening breeze. As he waded through the shallows back to the long strand of beach, he plunged the torch into the clear Aegean water. The fire went out with a hiss.

For thirteen months now, he and his father had explored the mysteries of the ship that had fallen from the stars. They had stepped through the gargantuan doorway opened by the long-dead sky-bull and ventured forth, tiny pools of light in the Stygian gloom of the ship's interior. It was not only dark but also twisting, and during one early expedition Icarus had become lost for a whole day, eventually stumbling out and into the arms of his relieved father.

After that brush with calamity, Daedalus had suggested a new strategy. The very next time they went inside, he first affixed one end of a length of golden thread to the entrance and unspooled it as they proceeded. That way, the explorers were able not only to return safely, but also to begin the process of mapping the interior. However, despite almost daily expeditions, after all this time they had plotted a mere fraction of the whole. Icarus had once compared the size of the ship to the king's magnificent palace at Knossos. To extend the comparison, if the ship was a palace then they had barely explored the outer wall. Doors that promised access to deeper parts of the ship frustrated all attempts to unlock them. Nevertheless, Daedalus's hopes of claiming a treasure trove of scientific discoveries had proved accurate, and the small portion of the ship they had exposed had indeed revealed wonders. All of these objects were currently stored in the cluster of low stone buildings lining the beach that Icarus was now splashing his way towards through the surf.

Needing a base from which to conduct their exploration, Daedalus had ordered a stone hut to be built as soon as the operation began. The king had granted workers to construct it and sentries to guard it. Meanwhile, Daedalus and Icarus began to fill the hut with marvels culled from the skyship. The first hut was quickly filled up, so a second building was commissioned. Soon, a collection of buildings had sprouted along the shore. As for the treasures themselves, as well as the flying device Daedalus had brought out on his first foray, they had since retrieved weapons, armour, tools and other objects whose functions remained a mystery. All had one thing in common – somewhere in their construction could be found the same small stone disc of interlocking gears. Daedalus had declared it a mechanical heart – the engine that drove the machines.

With a wary glance at the great bronze bull statue that towered over the entrance to the hut, Icarus passed inside. He didn't trust those things and wished his father had never created them. But it had been inevitable. One day, following an incident when the human sentries had fallen asleep at their posts, Daedalus had angrily dismissed them from his service.

'But how will we guard the treasure now?' Icarus had questioned him.

'We will make our own watchmen,' was his father's response.

Fashioning them after the likeness of the sky-bull that had perished on the day the ship crashed, Daedalus created statues of bronze, then brought them to life with mechanical hearts. Among his discoveries in the ship, he had come across the bull creature's language, written down on strange glowing tablets. Daedalus had deciphered enough of it to write a rudimentary set of instructions that allowed him to control the statues.

Icarus bowed his head under the low doorway and entered. The cool of the hut was welcome after the pulsating heat of the day. Music drifted across the room. His father played the lyra, bowing the strings on its pear-shaped body to create a melancholy tune. On seeing his son, he set aside the instrument. Icarus could tell by his expression that something had happened.

'The king has turned down my pleas.' Daedalus sighed.

Icarus understood instantly. Daedalus wanted only one thing from King Minos: more time to explore the ship. But the king had been sceptical from the start, terrified that his superstitious subjects would blame its appearance for failings in the harvest and any otherwise unexplained deaths. And then blame him.

'He orders it gone by sunset tomorrow.'

It seemed an impossible task, but they had prepared for this inevitability.

'Fetch Talos,' instructed Daedalus.

The soldier's name was Talos. He had slain the sky-bull and protected his king, but in its death throes, the bull had cursed him. Caught in an explosion, his flesh pierced by something smaller than an arrow's tip, his mind raced and his chest burned as if it contained the sun itself. From his bed, even through the haze of illness, he could hear the physician's words: the fever would take him in a matter of days. Then the old healer paused. Perhaps there was one who could help.

Daedalus took Minoan copper and combined it with rare metals from the skyship to forge Talos a suit of bronze. In form it resembled the bull the soldier had put to the sword. If Daedalus's calculations were correct, the bronze armour would draw the heat out of the man's body, like a salve that cools the sting of the scorpion. But, if he was wrong, then Talos would surely die. To Daedalus's relief, the suit did its job and, to his surprise, it revealed unique properties that he had not figured into its design. It enhanced Talos's strength, allowing him to lift heavy objects far beyond the power of an ordinary human. It made him swift too, and put the heat of a dozen forges at his fingertips. The soldier became the king's greatest weapon, defending the shores of Crete from his enemies with such strange vigour that there was an inevitability to his path: first they sang about him, then they wrote about him, and then he became legend.

Wooden scaffolding cradled the rim of the skyship. It had been tricky engineering the structure to remain steady on a base of shifting sand, but Daedalus had figured it out. He'd needed access to the top side of the hull to allow Talos to carry out the work. The bronze man kneeled on the surface, bent to his task. Daedalus had discovered that Talos's power to generate intense heat could be used as something other than a weapon. By touching two surfaces, he could melt them and, when they cooled, they were joined in a strong bond. Talos's fingers glowed as, under Daedalus's directions, he seared the skyship's skin.

Daedalus cast his eye across the completed work. Fused to the hull at more than a dozen places were great bronze wings. They appeared to have been clipped from some giant mythical bird. Daedalus, the master sculptor, had fashioned them in his workshop. They appeared delicate enough to blow away on the airiest breeze, which was not so far from the truth. At the centre of each was one of the flying discs found on the ship. Unable to scavenge enough of them, Daedalus had built his own, dismantling one of the originals to understand its working, then engineering a copy. Icarus had enjoyed testing the flying machine, soaring over the cliffs like a great sea-bird. The new wing worked perfectly.

'Where is he going?' Daedalus squinted at the great figure of Talos, who had descended the ladder and was now striding towards the skyship's entrance.

They caught up with him in the shadow of the ship, outside the huge doorway. Icarus gasped at what met them. There Talos stood, encased in his suit from toe to chest, but above his neck he was bare. He carried his helmet under one arm.

'You must put it back on,' said Icarus. 'You'll die.'

Talos gazed at the young man. 'It is enough.'

Daedalus nodded with grave understanding. The armour was not only his salvation but his bane. Imprisoned in bronze, it took a soldier's discipline to shield his mind from madness. A life enclosed in the suit was not to be endured indefinitely. Talos peeled off the remainder of the suit, turned his face to the sun and took a great gulp of sea air. He remained there a full hour. Then, taking his armour so that no other could suffer his fate, he boarded the skyship, sealing up the door behind him.

It was time.

Out to sea, dark clouds were gathering, black against the day, the storm far enough off so as not to disturb their mission. Daedalus and Icarus took up a position high on the beach, well back from the ship. Daedalus held one of the stone engines in the palm of his hand.

'Once you asked me how we should hide a mountain,' he said to his son. 'Now you shall see.'

'Father, may I?'

Daedalus passed the engine to him and Icarus set it going with a touch. Like the music of the lyra, its power reached out through the air. Icarus didn't understand how, but he knew that his engine was connected to all the other engines set into the wings.

One by one, they awoke, until their soft *tick-tick* mingled with the lapping of the waves.

The ship had tumbled from the sky and augered into the sand all those months ago, leaving half of its hull visible. Now the shining hull trembled. Slowly, the skyship rose into the air, sliding out of the sand like a sword being drawn from its scabbard. Borne by the wings Talos had joined to its surface, the skyship glided out over the water, towards the distant cloudbank. Seabirds followed it, squawking at the interloper in their midst. Far beyond the shallows, the ship altered its flight path, tilting up at an impossible angle so that, briefly, the daylight reflected from its polished disc as though the Earth had twin suns. Icarus shielded his eyes from the searing glare, squinting to see the outcome of his manoeuvre.

And then, for the second time, he watched the skyship fall.

The leading edge touched the water, breaking the surface with barely a splash, like one of the expert divers who leaped from the cliffs at Palaiokastro.

It slipped beneath the waves and was gone.

21. The Labyrinth Awaits

Aegean Sea, circa 2028 AD

The ship floated on the otherworldly blue of the Aegean Sea, waves breaking against its enormous bow with foaming bubbles, splashing the name etched on the prow: *Argo*. It was more than a hundred metres from stem to stern, stacked five decks high with a spire of communications equipment and two landing pads, one of which was occupied by a sleek helicopter painted in the Polichroniadis livery. Smart computer systems coupled to an old-fashioned anchor held the *Argo* in position with an error of plus or minus two metres. It rocked gently in the light wind, the gleaming white of its massive hull blindingly bright in the sunshine. This was the sea of legend, of Jason and the Argonauts, of Odysseus, and the ships that sailed here the stuff of myth. Yet, today, the smooth silence and unbroken blue was about to be disturbed by something older and even more mysterious. In the water at the prow of the ship, a fin appeared and then another, until an entire pod of dolphins had congregated. Whistling and squealing, two dozen snouts pointed skyward. It seemed as if they were waiting for something, their high-pitched fanfare heralding its arrival. A flurry of seabirds flew up into the sky with loud cries and a flapping of wings, circling and squawking.

A wheezing filled the air, and from out of the clouds came a small blue box spinning down towards the ship. With a final pirouette, it landed squarely on the largest deck, arriving with a hearty thud on the unoccupied helicopter landing pad.

The door to the TARDIS flew open and the Doctor bounded out, head bent over a device in her hand. At its centre was an Aénaos phone, but she had added a spiral antenna and enclosed the whole thing in a striking blue case that looked remarkably like a panel from the TARDIS's exterior.

Yaz was moments behind her. 'What is that thing?'

'Using the stone engine in this Aénaos phone, I was able to key it to the energy signature we've been following through time. This handset is monitoring the flow of energy from the future to the power plant in the present, tracking any fluctuations.' She pointed to a light on top of the case. 'Basically, when this flashes red, we've got about ten minutes before the planet explodes.'

Yaz eyed the device warily, half expecting it to start flashing, signalling the countdown to Armageddon. 'If we're going to find a cure for Ryan, we'd better get a move on, hadn't we?'

She glanced around at her new surroundings, taking in the opulence of the gleaming vessel. The TARDIS had whisked them through time and space to Greece and to the day after the events in the Swiss mountains. They had landed on a yacht belonging to the Polichroniadis siblings. On three sides, the blue Aegean stretched to the horizon. On the fourth, in the distance, lay the rocky outline of an island. This was Yaz's first trip to Greece. The summer after school ended, her friends had gone to Mykonos to see some DJ, but she hadn't been able to come up with the deposit. At the time she'd said she didn't care, although she did really; she had been crushed to miss out.

Under different circumstances, cruising the Greek islands on a ship like this would've more than made up for that disappointment.

Shading her eyes from the sun, she identified the command bridge set beneath whirling radar detectors and high-frequency aerials at the top of the ship. With its wraparound tinted-glass windows, the wheelhouse looked like a movie star pretending not to be famous.

'Nice superyacht,' remarked the Doctor.

With a sweep of her coat-tails, she made for the nearest gangway, her boots ringing off the metal steps as she began to climb. Yaz glanced back over her shoulder into the TARDIS. Graham had stayed behind to watch Ryan, whose condition was worsening. When Yaz left, he'd been pacing his room like a caged tiger, slamming his overheating body against the walls. She tried not to imagine the worst, but if he was going to survive, they had to shut down the energy drain from the future. The Doctor seemed confident that the solution was nearby. Yaz hurried after her.

Soon, they were almost at the command-deck level. It crossed Yaz's mind that they hadn't yet been challenged by any of the ship's crew-members. In fact, she hadn't seen a soul since leaving the TARDIS. The Doctor seemed to read her mind.

'Last time I was aboard a ship this quiet, it was the *Marie Celeste*.'

'Where is everyone?' asked Yaz.

'From what I've seen of Panos and Penelope, they tend not to trust the living. They prefer staff that can be controlled, preferably programmed. My bet is this ship is autonomous, with everything from navigation to putting those tiny umbrellas in cocktails handled by artificial intelligence systems. All you have to do is put your feet up and enjoy the scenery.'

There was at least one human aboard. They found Penelope alone on the bridge, a ship-to-shore radio pressed to her lips.

'Mayday, mayday, mayday.' She spoke urgently into the radio. 'This is vessel *Argo*. I require immediate assistance. My position is –' Catching sight of the newcomers' reflection in the glass window of the bridge, she spun round. Her usually cool attitude was briefly replaced by a mixture of surprise and relief.

'Doctor, you're here.'

'Well, I do like to be beside the seaside.' The Doctor strode across the bridge to inspect a bank of screens displaying what looked to Yaz like navigational information, including various maps and scrolling co-ordinates, none of which made the slightest sense to her. However, they clearly meant something to the Doctor, who immediately absorbed herself in the figures.

By contrast, on a desk beside the electronic displays was a set of paper charts, along with several items of ancient jewellery and pottery similar to the stuff Yaz had seen in the Polichroniadises' private museum.

White-faced and clearly shaken, Penelope stumbled. She caught hold of the edge of the control desk and steadied herself. Yaz went to help, but the other woman waved her away. 'I'm fine.'

'Yeah, you look terrific,' said Yaz. 'So, why are you calling for help?'

'My brother –' Penelope began, but then broke off, unable to continue. She gathered herself. 'He's down there.'

'Down where?' asked Yaz.

The Doctor pointed to one of the digital displays. 'Here, I imagine. This is a sonar plot of the seabed beneath the ship. And I'm guessing that bright green dot is where Panos went.'

'Display UAV images of target site,' ordered Penelope, and a set of photographs appeared on the adjacent monitor. They were pin-sharp and the colours so vivid that it was only after studying them for a few seconds that Yaz realised they had been taken underwater. Penelope magnified one of the images. The scale was hard to judge without any context, but it showed one half of a perfectly circular object, the other half embedded in the sea floor. 'We discovered this site a few months ago. Based on what we know of the stone engine's origin, we believe our best chance of finding a cure for Panos's condition is here.'

Yaz had difficulty summoning up much sympathy for Panos, but if he could be cured, then so could Ryan. She needed to know more about what they were dealing with. 'What is that thing?'

Penelope swiped through to another image of the same object, but from a closer angle. This picture showed a scuba diver, a tiny figure against what Yaz now saw to be a massive structure. There was a faint outline in the wide rim of the object. She peered closer, and realised it was the outline of a colossal door.

Finally, Penelope answered her question. '*That* is the entrance to the Minotaur's labyrinth.'

Yaz gawped. 'You're not serious.'

Penelope brought the other images into the centre of the screen. They were different from the first batch, not as clear and with some sections so dark as to be undecipherable. 'These are satellite images of the interior. We weren't able to penetrate as far as we would have liked. Amazingly, the exterior resists modern scanning techniques. But, as you can see from the little we have been able to map, the layout is –'

'Labyrinthine,' finished the Doctor.

The image showed a nest of twisting passageways so confusingly arranged that just looking at them made Yaz dizzy.

'We hired a team to explore the interior – the best people we could find. Panos led the team, but twelve hours into the mission I lost all communication with them. This is what I heard before it went silent.' She touched a control. There was a short delay, then Panos's voice sounded out across the bridge.

It took Yaz a moment to recognise him. The usually charming tone of his voice had been replaced by a hard edge.

'Karlsson and Niko are dead.' The next part was unintelligible. 'The walls . . . it was the walls . . . Continuing with mission.'

Penelope touched the control again. 'And this is his final transmission.'

The signal was broken, and only a few words were distinct through the static.

'Have penetrated to inner section . . . Talos! . . . Found it!' He repeated the last two words over and over. Through fast, shallow breaths he sounded exultant to the point of madness. Then the transmission cut out.

'Found what?' asked the Doctor.

'Perhaps the cure to his condition,' Penelope speculated.

'And what was that about Talos?' asked Yaz. When they'd rescued Ryan from the power plant, in his delirium he had rambled on about a lot of things, including the Talos project. But Yaz wasn't clear how his ravings connected to Panos's message.

'And the walls?' asked the Doctor. 'What is it about them, hmm?'

Penelope apologised, but she had no answers for them. She took a deep breath. 'I know this is a lot to ask of you after everything that has happened between us. But, please, help me get my brother back.'

Despite what she and Panos had done – kidnapping Ryan, their reckless pursuit of the Aénaos Engine technology – Yaz knew that the Doctor wouldn't refuse the woman's plea. In a universe of nos, the Doctor was a loud, ringing yes.

'We'll help you,' said the Doctor. 'But there's something you should know. It isn't the Minotaur's labyrinth. It's not even from Earth. That's a Nimon spacecraft.' The Doctor shook her head at her own failing. 'I should've figured it out before now. The technology in your Aénaos Engine – it's theirs.'

Penelope listened with growing astonishment.

'Funny thing, myths. You start off with a bull-like intergalactic species crash-landing on Earth four thousand years ago, whiz it up in the Great Magimix of Time, and voila! You get a monstrous bull lurking in the heart of a labyrinth and some truly lovely pottery.' The Doctor picked up a clay vase from the desk next to the monitors. It had a long neck and one broken handle and was decorated round the bulging middle with a faded picture of the Minotaur pursuing a young man.

Yaz sensed a breakthrough. 'So, if these Nimons are responsible for the technology, we can hop in the TARDIS and go ask them how to turn off their machine, right?'

'Sadly, no,' said the Doctor. 'You know the expression "like a bull in a china shop"? That's the Nimons for you – except the shop was their home world. They destroyed it and, having wrecked their own planet, went on to colonise another. Crinoth, it was called. Managed to burn that one to ashes too. No one's ever been able to figure out how they did it, until now.'

A shocked expression slid across Penelope's face as the full impact of the Doctor's words hit her.

'Looks like they wiped themselves out using what you call the Aénaos Engine.' The Doctor pulled out her customised handset. 'Let's try not to make the same mistake, shall we?'

'What is that?' asked Penelope warily.

'End-of-the-World-o-Meter,' said Yaz, turning to the Doctor. 'Please don't tell me it's flashing.'

The Doctor studied the screen. 'No, but it just registered a massive energy spike.' She glanced at Penelope. 'I presume you can communicate with every corner of your glorious empire from here?'

Penelope nodded and the Doctor asked her to raise the control room in the power plant in Switzerland. A few seconds later, the anxious face of an engineer filled one of the monitors. It was the same man who had been unable to deactivate the engine in the mountain.

'Hello again,' said the Doctor. 'I'm guessing that expression of fear and panic isn't because they ran out of Wiener schnitzel in the canteen.'

'Doctor, it's the Aénaos Engine. It's just as you said. We're unable to shut it down, and the engine is drawing so much power it's overloading. We can't stop it going critical.'

'How long before meltdown?'

'I may be able to slow the process, but if we can't shut off the flow of energy it's going to blow in less than two hours.'

No longer attempting to hide her alarm, Penelope turned to the Doctor. 'Can you stop this?'

'There might be a way.' The Doctor pocketed her home-made detector. 'But not from here.'

Yaz was puzzled. Hadn't they come here for just that purpose? 'From where, then?'

The Doctor turned slowly to regard the bank of monitors and the slow sweep of the sonar display.

'From the centre of the labyrinth.'

22. Dive! Dive!

Graham wasn't complaining, which worried Yaz, since he was currently being lowered into the roiling sea aboard a tiny submersible. It was the sort of situation usually guaranteed to elicit a cascade of objections from him. Instead, he sat quietly next to the fitful Ryan in one of the tightly packed rows of seats, as the launch system suspended them over the water. Not even the merest reference to an eighties Hollywood submarine movie or a Sean-Connery-doing-a-Russian-sub-commander impression escaped his lips. Yaz understood his silence only too well – he was deeply concerned for his ailing grandson.

Following the decision to go aboard the Nimon spaceship, the Doctor had suggested that Graham and Ryan remain in the TARDIS, but Ryan's worsening condition had forced a change to that plan. Graham had pulled the Doctor aside, out of the young man's earshot.

'He doesn't have long, Doc. He can't wait for a cure. So, if there's a chance something down there can make him better, I have to take him to it. Right now.'

The Doctor agreed. The means of saving Ryan and of saving the world was aboard the Nimon spacecraft. They gathered on the bridge to discuss the details of the mission.

'The power the Aénaos Engine is drawing through time is routeing itself through the Nimon craft,' the Doctor began. 'I'm going to reconfigure the systems aboard the ship to reverse the flow, effectively sending the energy back where it belongs: the future. That way, we rebalance the universe – it likes that. But first we need to get aboard the craft and make our way to the command deck.'

'Can't we use the TARDIS?' asked Graham.

The Doctor pursed her lips and said, 'Not this time. The same space–time disruption that knocked us off course when we tried to land inside the mountain in Switzerland is active in the Nimon vessel. Without reliable navigation systems, I can't get us any closer than we are now.'

'I know how to get us there,' said Penelope.

The lowest deck on the ship contained a tender bay full of smaller vessels. Alongside jet skis, a couple of launches and a powerful speedboat was a bright yellow submersible. It was one of two the ship carried – the other had already been called into service by Panos. It was about four metres in length and could carry seven passengers in its clear spherical cockpit. According to Penelope, the sub was designed to withstand the crushing forces of a deep dive and had multiple safety systems. Like everything else on the *Argo*, it was fully autonomous, but responded only to Panos or Penelope's voice commands. Which meant Penelope was coming on the mission, whether they liked it or not.

She slid herself into the pilot's chair. 'Hurry,' she called to Yaz and the Doctor. 'Get aboard.'

'I don't trust her,' Yaz whispered to the Doctor. 'She only cares about her brother.'

'You may be right,' said the Doctor grimly, 'but we don't have any other option.'

They climbed through the hatch and joined the others in the submersible. Yaz glanced back at Ryan. Secured in his seat by a five-point harness, his body spasmed, bucking against the restraints. Somehow, through the turmoil of his condition, he met her gaze and seemed to recognise her. His body became still for a second and a faltering smile appeared on his lips. He was still in there. Still Ryan. She smiled back.

With a hum, the rear wall of the tender bay began to open outward and down. Daylight flooded the electrically lit bay as the wall lowered to become a launch platform for the sub. In the ceiling was a track and a pulley. An arm holding the submersible moved along the track and swung it out over the open sea.

Penelope counted down. 'Launching in three . . . two . . . one.'

The catch holding them to the launch arm released and the submersible dropped into the water. Automatic systems trimmed the sub, sending it into a steep descent. On the helm, a display charted their depth and relative position to the Nimon ship. As the sub was buffeted by undersea currents, manoeuvring thrusters held their course steady. Yaz took one last look up through the clear canopy at the fading light from the surface. As they pushed through the gloom, Graham kept up a constant stream of chatter, talking to Ryan in a reassuring voice about everything from cars to football. Yaz couldn't help but be touched by the older man's concern for his grandson.

It didn't seem that long before a proximity alarm on the helm chirped.

'We're coming up on the target,' announced Penelope.

Yaz could feel the mood in the cabin alter. She tensed as, out of the blue, the vertical face of an undersea cliff appeared. With growing uneasiness, she saw that it wasn't a natural feature of the landscape, but in fact the rim of the Nimon ship. The submersible followed a preprogrammed path round its circumference. Halfway into the circuit, Yaz looked down through the cockpit canopy. Below them, murky blackness stretched into the deep. 'Uh, why is it so dark?'

'We're over a chasm,' said the Doctor. 'It appears the Nimon craft is resting on a ledge above it.'

Graham piped up from the seat behind. 'And when you say "resting", Doc . . .?'

'Teetering on the edge of the abyss might be a better description.'

'Oh, good.' Graham sat back. 'We wouldn't want this to be a walk in the park, would we?'

The submersible slowed as it reached its destination outside the colossal door that, until now, they'd only seen in photographs. Another small craft was already moored there.

'That's Panos's sub,' said Penelope.

It was identical to the one they were travelling in. It looked tiny against the vast hull.

With a puff of vectoring thrusters, their sub steered next to the other craft. Penelope peered into the cockpit and her face crumpled into a worried frown.

'I'm sure we'll find him,' said the Doctor, seeing her dismay at finding the vessel empty.

Penelope nodded uncertainly and ordered their submersible to commence its docking procedure. It fired its thrusters in short bursts, orientating itself to the door, before extending a hose from a docking collar round the submersible's main hatch. The hose reached out through the water, clamps securing it to the door, forming a watertight seal. There was a white flash as a plasma cutter on the end of a robotic arm bored a hole in the other ship's hull, creating a hatchway. The hose was about a metre in diameter – wide enough to crawl through – and Yaz realised with a gulp that this was their way in. There was no turning back now. One by one, they left the relative safety of the submersible and made their way along the temporary tunnel into the alien ship.

It was not what Yaz had expected. They'd brought breathing equipment and torches, but didn't need either. The ship hummed with power – courtesy, the Doctor explained, of the energy coursing through it from the future. The air was breathable, although it smelled musty, having until recently sat undisturbed for thousands of years. Light came from glowing panels in the ceiling, and offered a glimpse down the long passageway that stretched before them. The walls were rough grey stone carved with scenes depicting the bull-like Nimon race. In his transmission, Panos had tried to tell them something about the walls, but he'd been cut off. The scene next to Yaz showed a bloody battle in which an army of Nimons laid waste to an opposing humanoid army in spacesuits. As they set off along the passage Yaz noted similar scenes of carnage etched on the walls: here they slaughtered an insect race, there they butchered a legion of robot knights. It went on and on. The ship was one long history of Nimon conquests.

In the distance, Yaz heard a low grumbling sound. Some internal mechanism, she assumed. A few seconds later, it came again, but closer this time, and now it sounded like something heavy scraping across a floor. They paused at a junction.

The Doctor led the way as their little group pressed deeper into the ship. She seemed to know where she was going. Although, when Yaz thought about it, the Doctor always gave that impression, even when she was utterly lost. They came to a junction where the passageway forked and, for the first time, the Doctor hesitated.

'This way,' she said, stepping confidently down the right fork.

The phone call from the future flashed in Yaz's mind like a blinding headache. *Left, not right*. She reached out and yelled, 'No!'

It was too late. There was a flurry of scraping sounds just like the one Yaz had been hearing and she finally understood what was going on. The noise was coming from the walls. They were moving! They swiftly rearranged themselves, as if someone was shifting the pieces of a giant puzzle. Yaz could only watch in horror as, with a rasp of stone against stone, one wall slid between the Doctor and the rest of the group, coming to rest against the far side of the passage with a resounding thud, sealing her off.

The Doctor was gone.

23. Death in the Maze

Once the walls began to shift, they didn't stop. Sliding and swivelling, they swiped at Yaz, Penelope, Ryan and Graham like great pinball flippers. Yaz dodged one, then dragged Penelope out of the path of another before it could crash into her, but in doing so she found herself separated from Graham and Ryan. She caught the older man's eye just before the walls swung round again, cutting them off.

There was no way back to her friends.

Yaz hammered against the unyielding stone and called out their names, but they couldn't hear her through the dense material, or if they could they were in no position to answer. She'd messed up. Failed to carry out the Doctor's one crucial instruction. She wanted to sit down and cry, but she had to stay calm. Focus on the mission. Get to the command deck, trust that the others would make it there too. With her cheek pressed against the cold wall, she considered with some irony that, if there was one thing the Doctor had taught her, it was that the future wasn't set in stone.

She took a deep breath and stood back, and as she did so she noticed another scene etched on the wall: a Nimon battling three figures. Two were humanoid – a woman and a man with a floppy hat and what looked like a long scarf. The third was a small rectangular dog. Something about its geometric body suggested that it wasn't flesh and blood. A robot, then. Amazingly, the robot dog seemed to be keeping the much larger Nimon opponent at bay. For some reason, the picture gave Yaz hope.

'Oh no . . .' Penelope wailed.

Yaz turned to see the other woman launch herself along the passageway towards a crumpled heap. The shifting walls had revealed the limping figure of either Scylla or Charybdis, standing protectively over the body of a man, face down on the floor.

'Panos!' Penelope threw herself down next to the prone figure.

He was wearing black army fatigues and a backpack. A gas mask was slung round his neck and a submachine gun lay just out of reach of one rigid hand. Penelope heaved his body over to get a look at his face, all the while desperately repeating her brother's name.

Yaz put an arm round Penelope's trembling shoulders. 'It's not him.' She had to say it several times before the message got through. At last it dawned on Penelope, and she rocked back on her heels, sobbing with relief.

No tears for the unfortunate man, thought Yaz, looking down at his still body. Whoever he was, he was dead. The robotic dog hobbled to Penelope's side and she greeted it with a welcoming pat. Whatever had killed the man had damaged the dog, but it was still functional.

Penelope couldn't stop shaking. Yaz searched the dead man's backpack and found a water bottle. She unscrewed the cap and offered it to Penelope. 'Here, drink.'

Penelope sipped from the bottle and wiped her lips.

'Any idea who he is?' asked Yaz.

'I think his name is Jonas. He was a soldier – part of the team Panos hired to explore the ship.'

A soldier, yet his training hadn't helped him survive this death trap. What chance did she and the others have? Yaz pushed the uncomfortable thought to the back of her mind, where it could join all the others currently brooding there. Then she noticed that Jonas was wearing a small camera strapped to his head. She slipped it off and saw that it had a built-in screen.

'Maybe this'll tell us what happened to him,' she said hopefully. Anything to give them an edge. She set the controls to play the last few minutes recorded by the camera. A moment later, Jonas's face appeared on the small screen. Evidently, he had removed the camera from its headmount in order to video himself. He looked nervous, his eyes darting past the lens even as he talked into it.

'I don't know who's going to see this but, whoever you are, you need to know that it's not just the walls. There's something in here. It's hunting us down.'

Yaz glanced at Penelope. She was clutching the water bottle so tightly that it looked like it might crumple in her fist.

'Three of my team are already dead,' Jonas continued. 'I don't know what happened to Panos. We lost him somewhere in this hellish maze. Cole and I are the last.' From the recording came the distant chatter of gunfire. Jonas looked up at the sound, then back into the lens. 'Get out. Just get out now!'

*

The walls were closing in. Graham reckoned he had less than a minute before he was flattened between them like a cheese toastie. *Between a Breville and the deep blue sea*. Bracing one shoulder against the encroaching wall, he leaned in with a grunt of effort. A tiny part of his brain was telling him that maybe he could halt the crushing mechanism, but he couldn't hear it above every other part of his brain, which was screaming at him that he was going to die. Horribly. In about forty-five seconds. The leather soles of his shoes scrabbled for grip as the wall continued its inexorable slide towards him. Why did he always wear brogues? Why not trainers like Ryan? If he survived today, he swore he'd ask the Doc to fly the TARDIS immediately to the nearest JD Sports.

'Graham, how did you get yourself into this one?'

The answer to that was simple: the usual way. By following the Doc on a mission to save the world. Except this time it was more personal than that. He was here to save Ryan. The thought stabbed at him. *Poor Ryan*. Maybe it was the confusion caused by the moving walls, or the illness overwhelming him, but a few turns back Ryan had bolted and Graham hadn't been quick enough to catch him. By the time

Graham had roused himself, the walls had done their merry-go-round thing and he'd lost sight of the boy. Next thing he knew, he was stuck in this chamber of horrors.

This mission had started badly enough, losing the Doc almost as soon as they boarded the Nimon ship. Then Yaz, and then Ryan. Now Graham was all alone, facing the end. His foot slipped and he fell to one knee, slamming it against the floor. That was going to leave a bruise. With a wince, he realised that he almost certainly wouldn't be around long enough to see the bruise appear.

Hauling himself to his feet, he bent his shoulder once more to the wall and prepared to give one last heave. The ship had been down here for thousands of years, only springing to life in the last day or so. With a bit of luck, the ancient system powering the mechanism was more brittle with age than it appeared. A good shove might snap a lever, jam a wheel – anything to prevent what was coming.

But it seemed as if luck was the one thing they'd left behind on the surface. The walls inched closer together. Yeah, luck was putting its feet up poolside with a cocktail on Panos and Penelope's superyacht. Stuck in the narrowing gap, Graham took a deep breath and awaited the inevitable. At least that endlessly catchy song had stopped going around his head.

Graham!

He cursed himself. Why did he have to think of that? It was back – and now it'd be the last thing he'd ever hear.

'Ow!'

He shrank back from the wall in pain and surprise. It had suddenly become very hot. Steam rose in wisps as the moisture in the stone evaporated with the sudden temperature spike. He watched, fascinated, as the mottled surface changed colour, becoming red then white-hot. *Great.* As if being mashed wasn't enough, now he was going to be baked too. As he puzzled over this odd development, there came a faint grinding noise and then a hole appeared where his shoulder had been pressed. The size of a coin at first, it widened swiftly like an eye in the dark. From the other side of the wall came the ring of metal on stone, as if someone was striking it with a sledgehammer. All at once the wall came down in a tumble of stone and dust.

His way out.

Graham barely had time to catch his breath when he saw that he wasn't alone: broad as a barn door, bronze skin shining, a creature tilted its bull's head down to regard him with glowing eyes.

24. Here It Comes

Penelope was reluctant to leave the gun where they'd found it alongside the dead soldier, until Yaz pointed out that the weapon hadn't done him any good against whatever was prowling the corridors of the spacecraft.

The unpredictable walls shifted again. This time, once they had settled into their new configuration, Yaz could see what looked like a door in the distance. With a lingering glance at the unfortunate Jonas, she grabbed Penelope and ran down the passageway. Scylla trotted after them, its servo-motors whining. Yaz didn't know where the door led, or whether it would remain in sight long enough for them to reach it, but right now they were short of options.

'Something's coming.' Penelope's voice quivered as she cast a glance over her shoulder.

The words froze Yaz's heart. She had faced many terrors since joining the Doctor, but this felt different. This time, the Doctor was missing and Yaz was trapped hundreds of metres underwater in an alien spaceship. Over the scraping of the walls, she was aware of the steady thud of footsteps behind them.

'Don't look back,' Yaz instructed the other woman. 'Focus on the door.'

In her eagerness to reach the hoped-for safety, Yaz yanked Penelope along the corridor and immediately knew she'd pulled her off balance.

Penelope stumbled and fell, sprawling across the floor. She looked up in despair. 'We're going to die.'

'Get up!' Yaz yelled, heaving Penelope to her feet and setting off once again.

Penelope had twisted her ankle in the fall, slowing them down. The thudding footsteps drew closer. Scylla growled back down the passageway.

'Don't look,' Yaz urged under her breath. 'Don't look.'

They were almost at the door, close enough now for Yaz to see that it was a smooth metal panel twice the size of a regular door. With no handle. Panic rising, she scanned the surface again. Nothing. There was no way to open it. She felt her chest tighten and resorted to hammering with her fists, yelling at the cold metal.

With a *whoosh* the door slid straight up into the ceiling.

The two women and the dog stumbled through and, as they crossed the threshold, the door fell behind them like a guillotine. A moment later, there was a crash from the other side and the metal panel bowed inwards. Whatever was pursuing them was there. It threw itself at the door again, raising another dent.

'This would be a whole lot easier with my sonic.'

At the sound of the familiar voice, Yaz whirled round, flooded with a mixture of relief and astonishment. The Doctor sat cross-legged on the floor at the centre of what looked like an explosion in an electronics shop, attempting to join together a handful of components. She was alive. Yaz's mistake hadn't doomed her friend to an untimely Time Lord's end.

'I thought you were . . . gone.' Yaz meant forever.

'Disorientated, certainly,' said the Doctor. 'The shifting walls are a defensive system activated when the ship detects intruders. Highly effective.'

'Graham and Ryan are lost. I couldn't get to them,' Yaz said, her voice catching.

'Hey, this isn't on you, Yaz.' The Doctor jumped up and laid a comforting hand on hers. 'We'll find them.' She grinned. 'I have a totally brilliant plan.'

The hammering on the door continued and Penelope took a nervous step back. 'What is out there?'

'Nimon, of course,' said the Doctor. 'Don't worry. I've sealed the door for now. Should hold for another minute or two. Plenty of time.'

Nimon? That made no sense to Yaz. 'But this ship crashed four thousand years ago. Surely the crew are all dead by now?'

'Most of them are, but it appears that a handful survived, thanks to these.' The Doctor indicated a row of what looked to Yaz like jet-fighter cockpits arranged across the room. 'Hibernation capsules for interstellar travel. Keep the occupants in suspended animation for the duration of the trip, so that they can be revived at their destination, dewy fresh.' The Doctor frowned. 'Last time I encountered them, the Nimons had access to transmat technology for instantaneous travel, but I may have put them off using it, hence the old-fashioned starship.'

'How did you put them off?' asked Yaz.

'From memory, I sent them into a black hole. Still feel bad about that.'

Yaz inspected the first capsule. It was sealed, with a clear canopy enclosing a reclined chair. On the exterior, various wires and tubes were hooked up to a bank of monitors that displayed information in the same scratchy alien script she'd seen on the Sword of Aegeus. The chair was occupied by a creature with leathery black skin and a head that resembled a bull's. It was enormous, and suddenly the scale of the doors and passageways in the ship made sense to her.

'It's dead,' said the Doctor.

'Are you certain?' asked Penelope.

The Doctor nodded, continuing to work on the device she'd been assembling when Yaz and Penelope arrived. 'Dead as a dodo ...' She gave a thoughtful pause. 'Seems this capsule suffered a life-support failure during the crash.'

The dead Nimon wasn't what bothered Yaz. She was more concerned that the canopies on the next four capsules were all raised and the chairs empty. She drew her own unsettling conclusion.

'There are four of them out there.'

'My guess is three,' said the Doctor. 'If you figure that one must've been up and about four thousand years ago in order to start the Minotaur myth.'

There was a crash and a creak of straining metal, as the door bowed again under the pounding of the creature outside.

'So what's this plan of yours?' asked Yaz, an image of the dead soldier flashing through her mind. 'Are we going to blow that thing out of the airlock?'

'Yaz, Yaz, Yaz,' remonstrated the Doctor. 'We don't fling sentient life forms out of airlocks. Although, in this case – and I'm not usually one to judge – I would say we are dealing with a particularly nasty bunch. The Nimons have a history of stampeding through the universe, seeking out succulent populations and devouring them. Good job for Earth that this crew never managed to get a message back home, because you lot are *delicious*.' She brandished the new device she'd been working on. 'Right, this genius piece of improvised tech is ready.'

It looked to Yaz as though the Doctor had cobbled it together from parts scavenged from the hibernation capsules. And was that a chunk of stone from one of the walls? 'Uh, what does it do?'

'Lets me play at being Daedalus. Y'know, bloke who designed the maze in the story? Using this, I can take control of the corridors, and move them around any way I choose.' She marched to the door. 'I'm going to lose the Minotaur in its own labyrinth.'

Penelope's eyes widened in alarm. 'You're not going to open the door, are you?'

There was a rough hole in the wall next to the doorframe that looked like it had been made recently.

'Just need to couple this to the main defence system.' The Doctor slotted the device into the hole and secured it with a tangle of wires and clips. Then she twisted it ninety degrees, like a key. Moments later came the familiar grinding of shifting passageways. The Doctor bit her lip in concentration, turning the device back and forth several more times. 'Based on what I could dig up from the ship's systems, there are several escape pods located round the rim of the vessel. I'm rearranging the corridors to channel the Nimon to one of those pods before sealing it off. Once trapped, it will quickly realise that it has no option other than to launch the escape pod and leave Earth.'

Yaz took a moment to marvel at the Doctor's plan. Whenever possible, she would choose to defeat her enemy without causing bloodshed, even if it meant increasing the risk to her own life.

'Right, this should do it.' The Doctor turned the device one more time and the battered door slithered up into the ceiling. Yaz held her breath.

The Nimon was nowhere in sight. The Doctor had successfully reordered the walls. But the passage wasn't empty. Yaz squinted down the dimly lit corridor.

'Ryan!' she called out, running to meet him.

He was alone – no sign of Graham – but at least he was here. And alive. He collapsed in front of her and she stooped to embrace him, but the Doctor held her back.

'His body is radiating intense heat. You can't touch him.'

Ryan lifted his head and his parched lips formed a single-word question. 'Graham?'

Yaz hadn't seen him since they'd become separated. He could be anywhere on the ship. She knew it was unfair, but in his current state she had to offer her friend a crumb of comfort. 'I'm sure he's okay.'

'Graham, you're a dead man,' he muttered to himself. Confronted by the bronze bull monster that had broken through the wall, he'd ducked under its outstretched arms and fled along the mazy corridors of the ship, losing it in the cross-currents of moving passageways. He had been about to congratulate himself on his good fortune when he saw a shape lumber into the passage in front of him.

Another of those bull things.

However, this one was even bigger than the first, with a tough black hide, burning red eyes and two short but sharp-looking horns poking from its skull.

Skidding to a halt, Graham turned on his heel, only to discover that the first creature was blocking his route back. He was trapped between them. The Gold Knight in one direction; the Black Knight in the other.

Come on! Even Theseus didn't have two Minotaurs to contend with.

The Black Knight lowered its head, horns glinting under the lights. Graham didn't know much about bulls, only enough to guess that it was preparing to charge. To his surprise, instead of pawing its hoof against the floor and snorting, a pair of red beams flickered from the pointed tips of its horns. The wall exploded next to Graham, showering him with fragments of stone. The flickering lights were some kind of weapon. Death rays.

The Black Knight rolled its big head, lining up to fire another blast. This time Graham had a feeling it wouldn't miss.

There was a blur and he felt something speed past him, brushing his trouser leg. It was one of the robotic dogs belonging to the Polichroniadises. Spindly legs flashing, it bounded along the passageway and launched itself through the air at the Black Knight. The horns fired again, lancing into the robotic dog. Graham knew instantly that, if it hadn't thrown itself in the way, the deadly beams would have struck him. The robotic dog disintegrated.

Graham swallowed hard. He'd take his chances with the Gold Knight.

Heaving himself round, he began to run down the passage, only to see that the Gold Knight was already running full tilt at him.

This was it. The crushing walls hadn't killed him, but between them these two certainly would.

The Gold Knight was almost upon him. He could feel the intense heat emanating from its body. It caught him a glancing blow, sending him spinning against the wall. Then, to his astonishment, it swept past him and continued thundering towards the Black Knight.

The flash of death rays lit up the passageway, so bright as to force Graham to briefly turn his head. He heard a crunch of bone as the two combatants met and, when he looked again, he saw the Gold Knight had clasped the Black Knight in a bear hug, lifting the great beast off its feet. There was a terrible sizzling sound and a sharp, burning stench. The Black Knight howled, thrashing about in its opponent's unbending arms before becoming horribly still. The Gold Knight tossed it to the floor. It lay there, curls of smoke rising from its broken body.

Turning from its vanquished foe, the Gold Knight paced towards Graham, each step leaving a smoking outline on the floor. Graham scrabbled away, but knew it was futile. Every part of him ached and he was so tired. Only now, up close, did he see that the Gold Knight's skin was not just bronze in colour, but appeared to be some kind of metal armour. Placing one gauntleted hand on either side of its head, the Gold Knight removed its helmet, revealing a face he recognised all too well.

'Panos?' Graham blinked.

The man who stood there was definitely Panos, but something had altered deep within his personality, and when he spoke it was with a cold, magisterial voice.

'I am Talos.'

25. Eeny, Meeny, Miny, Moe

The command deck lay at the centre of the circular ship, a cathedral of alien technology. Yaz helped Penelope and the Doctor manoeuvre the stricken Ryan into an oversized chair, before taking a look at their surroundings. Designed for the colossal Nimons, Yaz felt what she imagined Jack must have on reaching the top of the beanstalk. A thick layer of dust coated the main operational stations: helm, weapons and communications. All unattended for four thousand years. Nevertheless, they sang with power. If she could have read the Nimon script scrolling continuously on a sweep of viewscreens, she would've known that, since coming back online in the last twenty-four hours, diagnostic routines had been checking the ship's systems eight hundred times a second. However, the diagnosis wasn't looking any better now than it had done the first time.

Propulsion: offline.

Life support: failing.

Hull integrity: twenty per cent.

And all of this dire information was being spewed on to the screens for the benefit of the only crewmember present. Not that he was paying much attention. In the centre of the bridge a command chair was occupied by the skeletal remains of another Nimon.

'I guess that's the captain,' said Yaz. 'He must've died in the crash.'

'She,' corrected the Doctor. 'You can tell by the shorter horns.'

'Aren't bulls male?'

'Nimons aren't bulls.' The Doctor studied the remains. 'Amazingly well preserved. Her ship looked after her all these years.' She gave the arm of the command chair a pat.

Despite the Doctor's melancholy tone, Yaz realised that this was a positive development. According to what they'd deduced from the hibernation capsules, there were three Nimons alive when they'd boarded the ship. The Doctor had used the moving walls to send the first to an escape pod. The captain accounted for the second.

'That leaves just one more,' the Doctor muttered. For the first time since the mission had begun, it felt as though the odds had swung fractionally in their favour.

The feeling didn't last long.

'What's that flashing?' Penelope pointed to a light on the dusty command-and-control console. Beneath a layer of grime, it blinked on and off. At the same time, the display on the central viewscreen changed, showing a camera feed of what appeared to be a hangar bay. The picture was grainy, but it was still possible to make out the stocky shape of a small craft. Its four engines started up in a pre-programmed order, a flicker of fire spitting from each exhaust nozzle in turn.

Yaz heard a distant roar and felt the hull vibrate.

'It's the escape pod,' said the Doctor, studying the picture intensely. 'It's launching.'

'That's good, right?' said Penelope.

Yaz agreed. 'It means your plan worked and the Nimon's taken the hint.'

'Yeeesss . . .' The Doctor stretched out the word uncomfortably.

'Doctor?'

'I may have miscalculated.' She pinched two fingers together. 'Just a smidge.'

The picture of the departing escape pod was obscured by smoke and fire. The video image broke up.

The roar of the pod's engines faded as it cleared the hangar and blasted off, but even after it had gone the command bridge continued to vibrate. There was a creak of straining metal and the ship moved, the deck tilting down at an angle that threw them across the bridge. Ryan was pitched from his chair and fell to the floor with a cry. Yaz caught hold of the edge of the nearest console and held on. The Doctor lost her footing, and her End-of-the-World-o-Meter tumbled from her pocket and skittered across the deck. It came to rest at Yaz's feet.

'The thrust from the escape pod's engines has disturbed the seabed,' the Doctor called from across the room, where she clung to the helm. 'The ship's slipping over the chasm.'

Yaz felt her grip weakening. 'What can we do?'

'Work fast,' said the Doctor. Slowly, she began to drag herself back up the canted deck towards the command chair.

'Scylla, fetch!' snapped Penelope. Internal gyroscopes compensating for the acute angle

249

and composite claws digging into the floor, the dog bounded towards the Doctor and extended a paw. She took it and allowed herself to be helped to the centre of the bridge. Apologising to the bones on the chair, she swept the skeleton aside and took a seat.

'Nice to have a chair with all the controls to hand,' said the Doctor, settling herself. 'I get knackered running around that TARDIS console.'

Yaz understood the basic problem facing the Doctor: she had to stop the energy flow from the future overloading the Aénaos Engine under the mountain, otherwise it would explode and take the planet along with it. But *how* the Doctor planned to do that went far beyond Yaz's comprehension. She couldn't help the Doctor, but perhaps she could ease Ryan's pain. Making her way slowly across the precariously angled floor to the spot where he had fallen, she settled next to his overheating body. Soothing words would have to do, for now.

The Doctor's fingers were a blur as they flew over the command chair's controls. Rather than the usual shimmering touchscreens, the interface was a row of chunky buttons and dials – a perfect fit for a stout Nimon hand.

'I'm bringing the Nimon ship's interstellar drive back online,' said the Doctor.

'You're planning to fly this thing?' said Yaz.

'I'm planning to blow it up.'

'I thought we were trying to avoid the whole explode-y scenario?'

'Blame Sir Isaac Newton. For every action, there is an equal and opposite reaction. When the main drive explodes, it should release enough energy not only to stem the flow from the future, but also to send all that energy back to its origin. That way, the universe will be perfectly rebalanced. Cue the victory parade, bunting and my modest acceptance speech as I receive Earth's Saviour of the Year award for the fifty-seventh year in succession. If you win it fifty-eight years in a row, they let you keep the trophy.'

Yaz could feel the ship slipping away beneath them. Detecting the outside threat, the systems switched to an external camera feed. On the viewscreen, the inky blackness of the abyss waited to devour them. How long before they toppled over the edge, she had no idea. She turned her attention to the Doctor, listening with incomprehension as she figured her way through the problem. Scientific formulae dense with obscure terminology spilled from the Doctor's lips like an incantation.

'Hmm.' Her fingers hovered over a switch.

'What is it?' asked Yaz, seeing her hesitation.

'I need to route the power through one of two conduits, but the system is telling me that one of them is damaged. Unfortunately, it's not telling me which one.'

'So try one, then the other?'

'No can do. It's a "cut the red wire or the yellow" kind of deal.' She wiggled her fingers. 'Eeny, meeny, miny –'

'Please tell me you're not resting the future of the planet on eeny, meeny, miny, moe?'

The Doctor's finger slid back and forth.

The future of the planet, thought Yaz.

The future . . .

And in that moment she finally understood the phone call from Doctor Then. It wasn't about going left or right in the maze. It was about this moment.

'I'm going to say right.' The Doctor's finger sank down towards the switch.

'LEFT!' yelled Yaz. 'IT'S LEFT!'

The Doctor drew up millimetres away from the selector. She threw Yaz a curious look and then, with a shrug, flicked the switch to the left. A second later a smile spread across her face. 'Whaddaya know?' She frowned at Yaz. 'No, seriously, what do you know?'

'I'll tell you later.'

The Doctor worked on, blocking out all distractions. After a minute or so, she slapped the arm of the chair in frustration. A portion of the viewscreen displayed a graph with a diagonal line creeping upwards. 'That's the predicted power output that will be caused by detonating the main drive. I've calculated it four different ways and the numbers don't add up. The explosion won't release enough energy.'

'What do we do?' Something flickered at the edge of Yaz's vision. She glanced down to see the Doctor's End-of the World-o-Meter on the floor next to Ryan and recalled it had fallen from her pocket during the first disturbance.

'Not sure,' said the Doctor. 'I need time to think.'

The light on top of the device flashed on and off. The destruction of Earth was imminent.

Yaz looked despairingly at the Doctor. 'You've got exactly ten minutes.'

26. The Second Heart

Graham had dreamed of the world ending. Back on the TARDIS, in the days running up to the discovery of the first stone engine, the dream had startled him from his sleep. He didn't think anything of it at the time, since he didn't believe in premonitions. Never bothered with fortune tellers at the fairground or played about with Ouija boards as a kid. But the dream had been so vivid: violent electrical storms, earthquakes cracking the continents, rivers running with blood. Real Old Testament stuff. At first, he had put it down to some particularly fine cheese they'd picked up from the Blue Caves on the planet Garbonzo (famed for producing the second most pungent cheese in the universe). But the events of the past few days had him reconsidering.

Had he glimpsed the future?

That was the thing about life aboard the TARDIS – you lost your sense of what was behind and what lay ahead. Time used to be a line Graham travelled from one end to the other, like the bus route he had driven every day for all those years. Or like the golden thread that girl strung through the labyrinth. So long as he clung to it, he'd always know which way was forward and which way went back.

He'd lost his grip as soon as he stepped aboard the blue police box.

But how could anyone travel with the Doc and not be affected? Stood to reason. He didn't have to believe in premonitions or fortune tellers. His dream didn't have to be a vision of the future. It was no comfort, but it was just as likely to be a memory of something that had already happened. Which meant that today, right now, somewhere in time, the world had ended.

But not Graham's world. Not if he could help it. Against all odds, he'd survived the maze and made it this far. The day wasn't over yet.

'Up here,' he said, waving at the bronze man heading off along a branching corridor.

Panos, or Talos – whatever he was calling himself now – turned round and lumbered back towards him. He looked like some kind of cyborg, Graham decided. Or a superhero. A man in a metal suit that gave him the power to burn through walls and defeat monsters.

From what Graham had been able to learn since the two of them set off together, navigating the twisting corridors in search of the others, the suit was thousands of years old, but more advanced than anything twenty-first-century technology could offer, even to a billionaire. The suit cooled Panos down by conducting his immense heat energy out through the bronze alloy. It was effectively keeping him alive. Which meant it would keep Ryan alive too. Unfortunately, there was just one suit – it was unique. And there was no chance of searching YouTube for a helpful how-to-build-your-own video.

When he'd first set eyes on the looming figure, Graham had feared the worst, but he'd got it all wrong. Panos had rescued him from the crushing walls, and then he'd put paid to the bull creature. So why didn't Graham trust him? Perhaps because, when Graham informed him about their mission, Panos had barely reacted. Did he even care that his Aénaos Engine threatened to destroy the planet? Panos had spoken fine words about saving the world, but maybe the truth was that he didn't give two hoots about anything except big yachts and mansions.

'Are you sure it's this way?' Panos asked, peering along the corridor.

'Trust me. This is our stop. Come on.'

The Doc had said the command bridge was located in the centre of the ship. The walls had stopped sliding around a while ago, giving Graham a chance to figure out a route there – but, not long after the corridors quit shuffling about, the whole ship had started wobbling. There was a distant rumble and a tremor shook them again. Bouncing from one side of the passageway to the other, he and Panos made their way to what Graham hoped was their final destination.

'Can't we boost the energy supply from somewhere else?' asked Yaz.

The Doctor didn't answer at first, but instead sat in contemplative silence for several seconds. Knowing how little time they had, Yaz guessed she was considering some momentous decision.

'Yes,' the Doctor said at last. 'From me.'

'What are you talking about?'

'Like humans, Time Lords are filled with blood and bone, but there's something inside us that you don't possess.'

'A second heart?' Yaz knew that Time Lord physiology was strikingly different in that way. She'd often thought about the Doctor's two hearts. One wasn't enough to hold the universe.

A small smile played about the Doctor's lips. 'And another thing. It's called artron energy – the secret not only to our time travel, but also to our longevity.'

'Then you can donate some of that, right? Like a blood transfusion?'

'But I can only access it under a unique set of circumstances,' said the Doctor, and in her voice Yaz heard a bell toll. 'When I regenerate.'

Regeneration was a Time Lord's last resort. It meant the Doctor would change physically, her consciousness transferring into a new body, her personality transforming too. Yaz had understood it in the abstract but, now that it was going to happen, she baulked at the thought of losing the woman sitting in the chair – she was *her* Doctor. But there was something else. She could see it in the Doctor's eyes. 'There's a problem, isn't there?'

'Call it a design flaw, but imminent death is about the only thing that'll trigger a Time Lord's regeneration. I have to be here when the main drive explodes.'

Yaz longed to unhear those words, to travel back in time and undo them. 'There must be another way.'

There was a distant wrenching of metal, and the Nimon spacecraft slithered closer to the edge of the abyss.

'Get to the submersible as fast as you can,' ordered the Doctor.

Yaz hesitated, her mind reeling. It had all fallen apart so suddenly. This really was the end. But how could Yaz leave her like this?

'Go!' the Doctor insisted. 'Get out now!'

'You're kidding, right?' Graham sighed from the doorway. 'We just flippin' got here.'

Yaz turned to see him standing next to a figure wearing what looked like a bronze suit of armour. The figure removed the helmet.

'Panos!' Penelope let out a cry of relief and ran towards her brother.

At the same time, Graham hurried to Ryan's side, deliriously happy to see him again.

Yaz observed their joy, deep in her own despair. Two reunions; one parting.

'I'm sorry,' the Doctor said to her sadly. 'It's been fun.'

'No.' Ryan hauled himself to his feet and began making his way unsteadily towards the command chair. Every word uttered from his burning mouth was an effort. 'The fragment in my eye . . . drawing energy like the Aénaos Engine.' He held out his arms to the Doctor. Blinding coils of electricity sparked around them. 'You need power. There's power inside me.'

'That's not happening,' the Doctor said. 'Forget it.'

'But I'm just Ryan Sinclair. You're the Doctor. You're too important to lose.'

'No life is unimportant,' the Doctor said coolly. 'Never say that again.'

'Let me do this. Please.' Ryan's voice faltered. 'I'm dying anyway.'

Yaz turned desperately from Ryan to the Doctor. She couldn't lose either of them.

'You're not dying,' Graham said fiercely. 'You can't.'

There was the clank of Panos's metal suit as he marched to the centre of the bridge and stood towering over the Doctor. 'You're in my seat.'

'Panos, what are you doing?' Penelope asked nervously.

'Protecting our homeland, sister, just as the story goes. I am Talos, gift of the gods, guardian of Crete. If it's power you need, Doctor, I have more than enough.'

The Doctor hesitated, clearly reluctant to vacate the chair and pass on the terrible responsibility. 'You don't have to do this, Panos.'

'Oh, but I do.' He smiled, and this time his usual charm was edged with something sadder. 'You don't think I'd let you take all the credit for saving the planet?' He gestured at her to get up and, when she didn't move immediately, he said, 'The difficulty is not so great to die for a friend –'

'As to find a friend worth dying for,' the Doctor finished the quotation.

'Nothing like a bit of Homer,' said Panos.

Slowly, the Doctor got up and he lowered himself into the vacated seat. He placed the helmet back over his head, sliding it into place and latching it on to the rest of the suit, sealing himself inside. The Talos armour immediately began to glow, turning the exterior from bronze to red.

The Doctor inspected the graph of the power output on the viewscreen. The diagonal line crept steadily upward. 'That'll do it,' she said.

'C'mon, let me help you.' Graham reached for Ryan, who shrank away.

'I don't want to burn you.'

'I packed aftersun,' said Graham, supporting his grandson with an arm. Together, they made their way off the bridge.

'Penelope,' said the Doctor. 'We have to leave. Right now.'

'Thank you, but no.' She said it as if she was declining an invitation to a garden party. She turned her back and walked over to her brother.

Yaz could see the Doctor weighing up whether to argue, but it was clear Penelope had made her decision. 'Let's go,' the Doctor whispered to Yaz.

At the doorway, Yaz glanced back at the brother and sister on the bridge of the alien craft. Her final glimpse of them was as Penelope lowered her head to Panos's, said something and smiled. Yaz would always wonder what it was.

'Anyone think to leave a golden thread?' asked Graham, preparing to enter the maze once more.

'Funny you should ask,' said the Doctor, pressing a button on her Daedalus device. Yaz watched as the walls of the maze reordered themselves once more. When they stopped moving they formed a straight line back out to the rim of the ship, where the submersible was docked. 'I figured we'd had enough labyrinths for one lifetime,' said the Doctor.

The corridor rocked as they raced along it, the ship inching inexorably towards the chasm. They reached the makeshift hatch and clambered through the docking tunnel into the sub. The

Doctor climbed in last, having first made sure the others were safely aboard. As Yaz took her seat, she remembered with dismay that the vehicle required voice control to operate. 'How are you going to pilot this thing?'

'If you can fly a Type Forty TARDIS, you can fly anything.' The Doctor grabbed the joystick and slapped at the controls.

The docking tunnel tightened as the Nimon ship slid further over the edge of the abyss.

'Go! Go! Go!' yelled Graham, cradling the overheating Ryan.

The submersible detached from the hull and angled up towards the surface, its thrusters firing.

Yaz glanced behind them at the colossal spacecraft. Overbalancing at last, one end tipped up like the giant fin of a sea monster. It hung there for a second or two before slipping away into the depths.

A moment later, there was a dull *whump* as its main drive exploded. The shockwave reverberated through the water, overtaking the tiny submersible, tipping it end over end. The Doctor calmly recovered the spin and pointed the nose towards the surface.

Almost immediately the joystick began to shake and the submersible veered off course. 'The sinking Nimon ship is causing a whirlpool effect,' the Doctor shouted above the sound of the sub's alarms. 'We're being pulled down.'

She flung the joystick hard to one side, guiding the sub to the edge of the sucking spiral of water. Yaz looked up. The water had been lightening as they climbed towards the surface, but now a great shadow appeared overhead.

Horrified, she realised what she was looking at.

'Doctor – the yacht! The whirlpool's dragging it down!'

'I see it. Hang on!'

The thrusters were already at maximum. The Doctor steered a course out from under the sinking yacht and the whirlpool's tow. It was going to be close.

Yaz held her breath as the prow of the *Argo* slid past the submersible and the yacht plunged into the depths. A terrible thought struck her, and she pressed her forehead to the canopy and whispered, 'The TARDIS . . .'

They breached the surface a few minutes later. The sea was calm and unruffled, with no evidence of the recent turmoil. The Doctor opened the canopy, allowing in a welcome draught of fresh air.

Ryan let out a cry, his whole body convulsing. Sweat poured down his face.

Graham sat up. 'Doc, we've got to get him to a hospital.'

With a moan, Ryan clutched a hand to his eye. He became suddenly still. When he drew the hand away again, something glinted in his palm. A tiny cogwheel.

'It's out,' he breathed in amazement.

'How're you feeling?' asked Graham, wide-eyed with hope.

Ryan thought about that for a moment, then said, 'Seasick.'

With a laugh, Graham wrapped him in a hug.

'May I?' The Doctor took the fragment of the stone engine from Ryan. 'This means the energy flow from the future has stopped.' She turned the tiny piece in her hand, the sunlight catching it for a moment. 'They did it.'

The four of them fell silent, reflecting on the sacrifices that had made this moment possible. Then the Doctor solemnly dropped the cogwheel over the edge of the submersible. It broke the surface of the water and quickly vanished from sight.

Yaz touched Ryan's forehead. 'Your temperature's already coming down. Now merely volcanic.'

'You know what all this has taught me?' said the Doctor.

'Oh good, a life lesson,' said Graham.

'μὴ τὸν θορυβώδεα κατσαβίδιν κάλλιπε,' said the Doctor, to blank looks from the others. 'Never hand over your sonic screwdriver,' she translated. 'First thing we're doing after this is making a stop in Switzerland.'

'Uh, hate to say it, but you might have a bit of a wait,' said Yaz. 'Forget the Alps. It's a long way to shore.'

The Doctor licked a finger and held it up to the wind. 'The destructive power of the Aénaos Engine has dissipated. Only a few echoes of the paradox machine remain. Just enough.'

'Enough for what?' asked Yaz.

The submersible bobbed in the silence, the only sounds the slap of waves against its hull and the cry of seabirds. *No, that's not quite right*, thought Yaz. There was one other sound.

A familiar wheezing drifted through the bright air.

Shading her eyes against the Aegean sunshine, Yaz watched the TARDIS appear, fading in and out of time and space, its lamp flashing. Finally, it materialised, hovering next to them, skimming the surface of the sea.

'Just enough time and space –' the Doctor turned to Yaz with a twinkle in her eye – 'to make a phone call.'

THE END

David Solomons is the best-selling author of the *My Brother is a Superhero* books, which have won the Waterstones Children's Book Prize 2016, the British Book Industry Awards Children's Book of the Year 2016 and the 2017 Laugh Out Loud Book Awards. He has been watching *Doctor Who* from behind a sofa since Jon Pertwee regenerated into Tom Baker. Writing *The Secret in Vault 13* and *The Maze of Doom* fulfils a lifelong ambition.

In addition to his acclaimed children's fiction, he has been writing screenplays for many years – his first feature film was an adaptation of *Five Children and It*, starring Kenneth Branagh and Eddie Izzard. He was born in Glasgow and now lives in Dorset with his wife, the novelist Natasha Solomons, their son, Luke, and daughter, Lara.

Beatriz Castro was born on September 19 1985, in Logroño, La Rioja, Spain. When she was a little girl, she was always either drawing or writing fantastic stories. She later studied at the School of Arts in Logroño.

After graduating in Illustration in 2008, she embarked on a career as a professional illustrator. Her books have been published by many international publishing houses: Anaya (Spain), Ediciones SM (Spain), Oxford University Press (Spain and UK), Usborne (UK), Harper Collins (UK), Auzou (France), and Rovio (Finland).

Beatriz's illustrations appear in textbooks, illustrated books and on covers. She loves making colourful images and funny character designs. She likes animals and books, classic stories and fairy tales, and she listens to rock and punk music.

ABOUT THE ILLUSTRATORS

George Ermos is an illustrator, maker and avid reader from England. He works digitally and enjoys indulging in (and illustrating) all things curious and mysterious. His recent works include the award-winning *Brightstorm* by Vashi Hardy, and *Malamander* by Thomas Taylor, which was a Waterstones Book of the Month.

A **SINISTER SCHOOL** where
graduation means death . . .

A **MONSTROUS MYSTERY**
lurking beneath a quiet
London street . . .

A desperate plea for help
delivered by – hang on . . .
A POTTED PLANT?

The first thrilling, hilarious and scary adventure
for the Thirteenth Doctor,
by David Solomons.

THE BEGINNING

Wait – you didn't think that was it, did you?

Puffin has **LOADS** more stories for you to discover.

Find your next adventure at **puffin.co.uk**, along with:

- **Quizzes, games and apps starring your favourite characters**
- **Videos, podcasts and audiobook extracts**
- **The chance to check out brand-new books before anybody else!**

puffin.co.uk

Psst! You can also find Puffin on PopJam